CHILD *of the* MOUNTAINS

CHILD *of the*

MOUNTAINS

marilyn sue shank

A YEARLING BOOK

Sale of this book without a front cover may be unauthorized. If the book
is coverless, it may have been reported to the publisher as "unsold or destroyed"
and neither the author nor the publisher may have received payment for it.

This is a work of fiction. Names, characters, places, and incidents either are the
product of the author's imagination or are used fictitiously. Any resemblance to
actual persons, living or dead, events, or locales is entirely coincidental.

Text copyright © 2012 by Marilyn Sue Shank
Cover art copyright © 2012 by Richard Tuschman
Map copyright © 2012 by Joe LeMonnier

All rights reserved. Published in the United States by Yearling, an imprint of
Random House Children's Books, a division of Random House, Inc., New York.
Originally published in hardcover in the United States by Delacorte Press, an
imprint of Random House Children's Books, New York, in 2012.

Yearling and the jumping horse design are registered trademarks of
Random House, Inc.

Visit us on the Web! randomhouse.com/kids
Educators and librarians, for a variety of teaching tools,
visit us at RHTeachersLibrarians.com

The Library of Congress has cataloged the hardcover edition of this work as follows:
Shank, Marilyn Sue.
   Child of the mountains / Marilyn Sue Shank. — 1st ed.   p. cm.
ISBN 978-0-385-74079-1 (hc) — ISBN 978-0-375-98929-2 (ebook)
ISBN 978-0-375-98969-8 (glb)
 [1. Secrets—Fiction. 2. Families—Fiction. 3. Self-reliance—Fiction.
4. Christian life—Fiction. 5. Schools—Fiction. 6. West Virginia—
History—1951—Fiction.]   I. Title.
   PZ7.S548413Ch 2012   [Fic]—dc23   2011026174

ISBN 978-0-375-87331-7 (pbk.)

Printed in the United States of America
10 9 8 7 6 5 4 3 2 1
First Yearling Edition 2013

Random House Children's Books supports the First Amendment
and celebrates the right to read.

To my brother, Tom Shank,
and in loving memory of my father, Joe Shank,
and my mother, Lenuh Shank—proud West Virginians
who gave me reason to value my heritage.

And to all children of the mountains: "Rise and shine!"

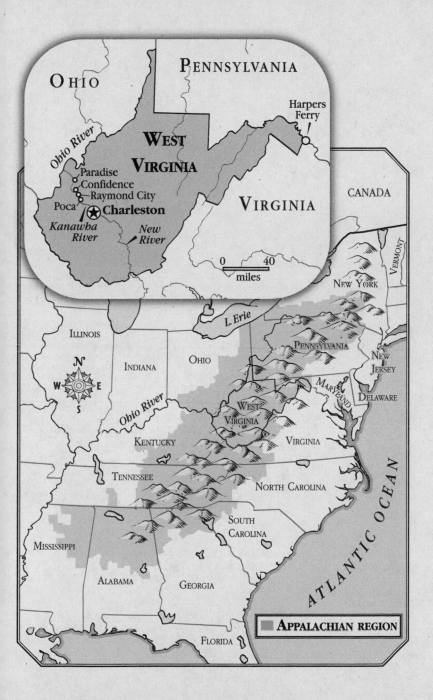

These women of Appalachia, they didn't survive.
They prevailed.   —*Margaret Hatfield*
                    from the West Virginia History Film Project

1

It's about my problem.

My mama's in jail. It ain't right. Leastwise, I don't think so. Them folks that put her there just don't understand our family. My mama's the best mama in the whole wide world. Everbody used to say so afore the awful stuff happened. Even Uncle William. And he don't say much nice about nobody.

I got to get her out. But how? Even when they's wrong, once grown-ups make up their minds about something, a kid like me don't stand much of a chance of changing it. Poor Mama. I know she hates being caged up like a rabbit, and it's all my fault.

I feel like my heart done shattered in tiny pieces, like Gran's vase that me and BJ broke playing tag one time.

And I ain't got nobody to help me put them pieces back together.

That's why I stopped by the company store after school yesterday and bought me the biggest spiral notebook they had. Maybe writing everthing down will help me sort it all out.

"Lydia, when you came to be, you was my only star in a dark, dark sky," Mama always said. When I lived in Paradise, Mama and Gran always made me and BJ both feel like we was right special to them.

But sometimes a body can feel all alone, even when other people live in the same house. That's how I feel living with Uncle William and Aunt Ethel Mae here in Confidence, West Virginia. They be nice enough people, but they ain't got nary a clue about what to do with me.

The bad stuff commenced like this: My brother, BJ, was borned awful sick, but we didn't know it at first. When Mama birthed me, Gran said I didn't cause Mama no trouble at all. Daddy was at work, so Gran hollered to a neighbor across the road that I was a-coming soon. The neighbor got in his car and went to fetch old Doc Smythson.

When Doc Smythson comed to help Mama, Gran told him she could manage things just fine, but he said he would be awful obliged iffen she let him help because it was his doctoring duty. So Gran figured it would be okay. But Gran told me that she really done most of the work, after Mama, of course. Gran midwifed most of the women around these parts. She fixed Mama blue cohosh tea to sip and tickled her nose with a feather.

Gran said, "When your mama sneezed, you whizzed out of her like a pellet from a shotgun. All Doc Smythson had to do was hold out his hands to catch you." Gran shook her head. "Ain't like you have to go to some fancy school to learn how to do that!"

But things sure turned out different with BJ. I recollect the whole thing. I was four years old at the time. Gramps and Daddy lived in Heaven by then. Me and Mama and Gran lived in Gramps' cabin all by ourselves.

When BJ was about to come, Mama started bleeding real bad, and she screamed like a hound dog a-howling at the moon. Nothing Gran mixed from her herb bottles helped none. Gran sent me running to the neighbors' house to have them find Doc Smythson.

Doc took one look at Mama and told Gran he had to fetch her to the hospital in Charleston straight away. But we didn't have no ambulance close by where we lived. Sometimes the men from the funeral home took folks to the hospital in their hearse. But they couldn't get to our house soon enough for my mama, tucked way back up in the mountains as we are.

So Gran wrapped Mama up in blankets, and Doc carried her like a sack of taters to his jeep. Her eyes was closed like she was asleep. I cried out to her, "Take me with you, Mama! Take me with you!"

She opened her eyes just a little and looked at me. Her

lips said, "I love you," but no sound come out at all. Doc sped off with her to the big hospital in Charleston.

Tears commenced to roll down my cheeks when I watched them drive away. Gran smoothed the hair back from my face with her hands, rough as a cat's tongue. "Your mama needs us to stay here and look after things for her, pumpkin," she said.

When me and Gran went back inside, Gran pulled Mama's bloody sheets offen the bed and took them to the washtub. I couldn't bear to watch the water take Mama's blood away, thinking that was all I had left of her. So I runned under the kitchen table and curled up like a woolly worm that somebody poked with a stick.

After Gran got done a-scrubbing and a-hanging out the sheets to dry, she leaned under the table and took my hand. "Come on, child," she said. "Your mama needs us to be strong for her. Besides, I ain't got the bones for bending down like this. You ain't helping your mama none by hiding under the table. Let's fix up the cabin all nice for her and the baby to come home to." I crawled out, and Gran handed me a little broom Daddy made for me afore he died.

I got myself busy sweeping the floors ever day Mama stayed at the hospital. Gran said, "Lydia, I declare, you're going to wear holes in the floor clean through to Chiny iffen you keep that up." But I wanted them floors to be spanking clean for my mama.

Mama finally comed back and brought my new baby brother with her. Gran folded up a blanket and laid it in a

4

dresser drawer on Mama's bed for him to sleep in. It made me think of Baby Jesus in the manger to see him lying there all cozied up.

Mama named my brother Benjamin for my grandpa on Daddy's side and James for my gramps on Mama's side. But he looked just too little to be Benjamin James. I wanted to call him Ben Jim, but Gran said, "Mercy, pumpkin, that sounds more like the name of a tonic than a fitting name for a boy. I can hear it on the radio now. 'Ben Jim heals your soul and heart, mends your body and makes you smart, keeps you strong and cures the farts.'"

So we took to calling him BJ instead.

BJ looked as cute as a speckled steamboat on a spotted river, as Gran used to say, even iffen he was as skinny as a straight pin. He had big blue eyes the color of our pond when it froze over. Them eyes looked clean through you, right inside to your very soul. His hair was the color of a ripe ear of corn. I used to hold him on my lap and tell him stories—about our daddy, about living up here on the mountain, and about how much we all loved him. He'd look at me and grin, and this little dimple would creep up like an extra smile.

Sometimes I'd think he sure lucked out being that cute. All I got was plain brown hair, plain brown eyes, and a plain face. And a bunch of awful freckles. I asked Mama, "How come I didn't get blue eyes like BJ?" She said, "You got soft, gentle doe eyes instead, Lydia. Eyes just like your heart." I felt better after that.

BJ was so tiny he made me come to think of *Tom*

Thumb—a story Gran used to tell me about a little boy the size of his daddy's thumb. BJ mewed like one of our old cat Hessie's kittens when he wanted a drink from Mama's breast. His sucking sounded like purring almost. Sometimes I wished that I could curl up with Mama like that—all safe and warm. But I thought I was too big because Mama was so weak. Feeding BJ seemed about all she could manage. So I didn't ask. Besides, I had to help Gran with the cooking and other chores. I didn't mind so much. I pretended I was all growed up and a real important person.

One day while Mama slept, Gran let me hold BJ for the very first time. I had to sit in the rocking chair and be real careful. His neck still flopped about like my rag doll. I curled my arm around him when Gran laid him in my lap. He didn't weigh much more than a mess of green beans. I looked down at his big eyes, and he looked up at me. "Looky there," Gran said. "He's a-smiling at you."

I smiled back at him. I knew right then and there that I was somebody special to my baby brother. "I will always take good care of you, BJ," I promised in a whisper only he could hear. "Always and forever. I won't let nothing bad happen to my BJ."

I tried real hard to keep that promise, but I couldn't. Gran always reminded us when something bad happened that the rain falls on the just and the unjust. The rain that Gran talked about sure poured down mighty hard on our family.

2

It's about missing home and them girls at school.

Folks around here know the tale about Mama and BJ—at least they think they do. Them big-city newspapers wrote about Mama's story, but most people heard tell of it from someone shooting their mouth off. Ain't none of them got it right, though.

When Mama went to jail, I had to come live with Uncle William and Aunt Ethel Mae in their shotgun house at the coal camp in Confidence. Gran once told me that Uncle William's house is called a shotgun house on account of iffen you shot a pellet at the front door, it would fly clean through the whole house and out the back door.

Mama thought different. "Lydia," she said, "it's a

humpback house, on account of having a room on the top. Your uncle has a bigger house than most of them coal miners. He's a boss over some of them men." Mama held her head real high when she said that. I know she's right proud of her brother. That little room upstairs is where I sleep. At least it has a window, so's I can look at the stars at night.

The house is painted white and has green shutters on the windows. You walk up three steps to the porch. Then you walk in the door to the living room. Aunt Ethel Mae likes to decorate everthing with flowers. She has wallpaper with flowers, pictures of flowers, and a floral couch cover. She even has fake flowers in a vase painted with flowers. Sometimes she sprays them with perfume. I don't know why she don't just grow her some real flowers in her yard. I guess she didn't think about that. For some reason, I always feel itchy when I sit in that living room.

When you go through the living room door, you find yourself in Uncle William and Aunt Ethel Mae's bedroom. They's some stairs in their room that lead up to my room. When you go through their bedroom door, you're in the kitchen. A little bathroom sits off to the side. Out the kitchen door, they have theirselves a tiny stoop and yard.

I sure do miss living in the house that Gramps built with his own two hands. My great-grandpa deeded him the land when he first got married. Gran loved to tell stories about the house that started off as a little cabin. She said Gramps called it his make-do house. That's on account of him making do with whatever supplies he could find to build it. Each time he had another young'un, he made do by adding another room. When him and Gran first got married, the cabin had one big room that they used for sitting, cooking, eating, and sleeping. He built a johnny house out in back for the other stuff folks got to do. Gran said he made it a two-seater so's she could feel rich.

When they been married for a year, Gran told him, "It sure would be nice to have us a place to sit in a swing and look out over the mountains of an evening." So Gramps created her a front porch and his swing still hangs from two chains today.

When they been married two years, Gran said, "It sure would be nice to have a place to sleep so's people wouldn't have to stare at our bed when they come to set a spell." So Gramps created her a bedroom on the top of the house.

When they been married three years, Gran said, "It sure would be nice to have a room for this young'un that's a-coming in a few months." So Gramps created Uncle William's room on the left side of the house.

When they been married five years, Gran says, "It sure would be nice to have a room for this new young'un that's joining us soon." So Gramps created Mama's room on the right side of the house.

Gran couldn't have no more babies after Mama, but that weren't the last of them room addings-on. Gran thought it sure would be nice to have herself a sewing room and a dining room over the years, too. My gramps loved my gran a awful, awful lot. So Gramps created them rooms, the kitchen on the back of the house, the sewing room on top of Uncle William's room, and a dining room beside the kitchen.

When all them rooms was done, Gran said, "It sure would be nice to have this whole entire house painted. You know, so it could blend into the sky." Gramps knowed that meant she wanted it painted blue, her favorite color. So sure enough, Gran got herself a blue house.

Gramps died when I was only three years old. I don't recollect much about him, just him tickling me with his long white beard. And I have a foggy recollection of him carrying me outside on his arm. He pointed out birds and twittered their calls. He smelled a little musty, but I have a warm, soft feeling when I think about him. Mama told me Gramps called me Sparrow on account of my brown hair and freckles. I like that.

After Gramps died, Daddy said we would move in with Gran to help her out. When I think on it now, I wonder iffen Daddy moved us there to help *him* out. Him and Mama had been renting a tiny house in Raymond City.

Gran was getting too old to climb them rickety stairs, so she took Uncle William's old room. Mama and Daddy slept in the upstairs bedroom. Mama fixed up Gran's old sewing room for BJ. She mixed up some paste and wallpapered the room with the Sunday funnies that Uncle William saved up from the *Gazette*.

I slept in Mama's old bedroom. It was painted a light peach color. My bed was covered with the quilt Gran made for Mama when she was a little girl. She used all different colors of floral materials to make a Sunbonnet Sue pattern. The quilt smelled like Gran and Mama close together, and I always felt safe tucked in under it.

I loved the tin roof that Gramps put on that little room when he created it. I liked to listen to the rain tinkling and pattering. Ain't no better song than that to lull a body to sleep.

Sometimes BJ and me spent time sitting on his bed looking at the hills and sky out his upstairs bedroom window. Ain't no better picture for a wall than that 'cause God Hisself painted our picture, and it changed ever day.

When I think about Gramps' make-do house, I always recollect the smells. Gran's room always smelled of lavender. Daddy and Mama's room smelled of whatever fresh flowers and herbs was a-growing in the woods. And the kitchen always smelled of yummy surprises when I walked in from school. Chicken and dumplings, my favorite. Pinto beans and corn bread. Ham and fried apples. Meat loaf with ramps and fried taters. Buttermilk biscuits. Oatmeal and molasses cookies.

It weren't no fancy mansion like a lot of city folks have. But there ain't no better house in the world than Gramps' make-do house on account of that house being home.

I don't think Uncle William's house will ever feel like home. Mama always said Uncle William is the strong, silent type. He's sort of scary, I think. He has blue eyes, but they look hard like steel, not soft and glittery like BJ's and

Mama's. He wears his light brown hair cut short and sticking up on top like he's still in the army fighting the Nazis. He would pat me on the head sometimes when I was little, but I always thought it was best to stay out of his way as much as I could.

Aunt Ethel Mae has hazel eyes and black hair that she tries to fix like some of them movie stars by using bobby pins to push it in a roll around her face. Then it falls smooth and curls under in another roll at her shoulders. She wears bright red lipstick and uses a eyebrow pencil to paint a mole aside her mouth. I don't like the mole I have on my arm. I can't figure why anybody would want a fake one, but she calls it her beauty mark.

Aunt Ethel Mae's real slender, almost skinny, and she's taller than Mama. My aunt smells sugary sweet with some cigarette smoke mixed in. She's always grinning and laughing real loud when she's with other people. But when she's in this house, her face looks tight and kind of sad.

Moving in with Uncle William and leaving Mama, my house, my old school and friends hurt bad enough. But the very worst part was not being able to leave them secrets about Mama and BJ behind, too.

Yesterday, some of them girls at school soured the air talking about BJ. Most times, I take a book to read at recess and sit under a tall elm tree as far away from them other kids as I can get. Now that them gold and brown leaves have fell to the ground, I have me a cozy, crinkly nest to sit in.

Iffen them girls start up playing a game, sometimes

12

they'll just let me be. But not yesterday. Cora Lee, Maggie, and Penny tired out of playing hopscotch and walked over to me. I tried real hard to keep reading my book, *Anne of Green Gables.*

Cora Lee—she always starts stuff. She thinks she's special on account of she's got a pretty face, blue eyes, and long black hair that curls at her waist. Her father works as a big shot at the coal company. They used to live in Pennsylvania, and she talks different. She has ten store-bought dresses. I didn't have to count. She brags about them all the time. She never wears the same dress two days in a row. Them other girls follow her around like she's a bitch dog and they's her puppies. I could feel Cora Lee's grin without looking up at her. "Hey, child killer's daughter," she said. "Whatcha reading?"

"I bet it's a murder mystery," Maggie said. She twisted one of her long blond pigtails in her fingers. I kept thinking how I would like to pull them both and tie them in a knot.

Penny leaned in close to me. I could smell her stinky breath. "It's Halloween," she said. "Do you think BJ will come back as a ghost and haunt you?"

Keep reading, keep reading, keep reading, I told myself.

Anne Shirley didn't have no one to help her out neither. But she always stayed real strong. She never ever let no one mess with her. I bet she would have told them girls, "When you go trick-or-treating, you all ain't got to wear no masks, you ugly monsters!" Excepten Anne would have said it all fancy.

But I ain't like Anne. I felt myself shrivel up like a morning glory when the sun leaves the sky. My skin got hot. My fingernails gripped the book so tight that I made little ridges in the cover. I turned a page that I knowed I would have to read all over again later.

"Come on," Cora Lee said to them other girls. "Who cares what she has to say anyways?" They laughed and prissy-pranced their way back to the other kids, just as my teacher, Mr. Hinkle, walked out the door and rung the bell to go inside.

To tell the truth, I don't know how much more I'm going to be able to take. One time, I tried to tell Aunt Ethel Mae about them girls. She commenced to crying when she heard the mean stuff that they said about Mama. I don't tell her no more. I don't want her to have to feel bad, too. But when I got home today, a few tears snuck out of my eyes when I walked through the door. She saw them, even though I tried to sniff them back inside as quick as I could.

After supper, Aunt Ethel Mae started a-preaching at me while she runned water in the sink for the dishes I cleared from the table. "Honestly, Lydia, you ain't been eating enough to keep a bird alive. Now, there ain't no use getting yourself all worked up and in a tizzy over them girls at school. They ain't got a lick of sense anyways. They should ought to mind their own business. Here," she said as she shoved a bowl of Tootsie Rolls at me. "Make yourself useful tonight and get your mind offen your troubles. Pass out this here candy to the trick-or-treaters."

Out of the corner of my eye, I saw Uncle William giving me the hairy eyeball from his chair in the living room as he crocheted another afghan. I ain't never seen any man afore Uncle William crochet. He used to give some of them afghans to Mama to take to church for people in need. I asked her about it one time. She said Gran taught him how to crochet when he was little to keep him out of mischief. "Idle hands is the devil's workshop," she told him. For some reason, he decided he liked it, I guess. He sure has made a bunch of them.

Uncle William listened to *The Aldrich Family* on the radio while he crocheted, but I knowed from that look in his eye that he heard ever word Aunt Ethel Mae said. And I also knowed I best do what she told me without no backtalk.

I swallowed the hurt that was a-churning in my stomach like butter and took the bowl. I wish I could be like Anne. Anne would have told Aunt Ethel Mae that she ain't got the sense God gave a scarecrow for telling me to hand out candy to kids the same age as BJ when he passed on. I would have to be nice to them little kids. It weren't their fault.

Instead of going to bed like I wanted to, I headed for a chair in the living room to wait for the first knock on the door. Soon I stood on my feet more than I sat down, a-passing out candy to cowboys, Indians, and princesses.

"Trick or treat!" the kids shouted, their grinning teeth peeping out from homemade costumes.

"Them costumes is great," I said, trying to keep my

eyes away from their faces as much as possible. It worked for a while.

But then it happened. A little boy wearing a tattered old sheet with a hole for his face smiled at me and his blue eyes seemed to laugh. His two front teeth was missing, just like BJ's on the day he left us. The tears wouldn't stay locked up in my eyes no more.

Aunt Ethel Mae saw me as I shut the door. "Oh, honey," she said. "I'm so sorry. What was I thinking?" She tried to put her arm around me, but I pulled away and runned to bed. She weren't thinking. That be the problem. Mama would have knowed better.

I buried my head in my pillow, but all the bad stuff—losing Mama and BJ and Gran and Daddy—washed over me like floodwaters.

"I wish you would send BJ back as a ghost to haunt me," I whispered to God. "I sure do miss him."

3

It's about my daddy.

Thursday, November 5, 1953

I wonder how come sometimes you love someone and hate them at the same time. I can't figure out how my heart can hold all them good and bad feelings about my daddy. I had me a nightmare about him again last night.

Daddy never even got to lay eyes on BJ. My daddy got killed when he went on a construction job at a church in Poca three months afore BJ come along. Mama saved the newspaper article about what happened. I used to get it out of the family Bible and read it sometimes. It says that Daddy died when a wall they built to hold back the dirt for the basement caved in. The loose dirt and cement blocks fell right on top of him. They couldn't dig him out in time to save him. Uncle William always says he's surprised it weren't him that got swallowed up by the ground, working in the coal mines as he does.

I hate to think of Daddy being buried alive like that. I still get the nightmares about it a lot. I wake up shivering—cold and hot at the same time. My breath gets swallowed up inside me, and I scream, "I can't breathe! I can't breathe!"

When I got the nightmares at home, Mama would sit beside me on the bed, stroking my hair and cooing to me, "Shhh, Lydia. It's all right, baby." Then she would sing, *"His eye is on the sparrow, and I know He watches me."* Sometimes Gran would bring me a cup of chamomile tea.

But when I woke up screaming last night, Uncle William just yelled from his bedroom, "Be quiet in there, Lydia. You're having another bad dream is all. I got to get up at four o'clock. Now turn over and go back to sleep." I think Aunt Ethel Mae slept through the whole thing.

I turned over like Uncle William said, but sleep never comed back. I finally got up and sat by the window. The stars seemed to wink like they was a-telling me they knew my secret but wouldn't never tell a soul. I wondered iffen Mama could see the stars winking at her through the bars in her cell window.

Sometimes I have nice dreams about the good times with Daddy. I can smell the sweetness of his chaw and the warmth of his sweat after he worked hard all day. I help him saucer and blow his coffee after he washes up and sits down to supper. Mama pours him a boiling hot, steamy cup when he finishes eating. He pours some of it into the saucer and adds a little cream. Then he winks at me. I come running over and help him blow on it to cool it off. He slurps it down from the saucer. Then we look at each other and say, "Ahhhhh, now, that's good coffee!" He pours some more coffee in the saucer, and we start all over again. When he's done, he picks me up in his strong arms and swings me around while he sings:

> "Old Dan Tucker was a mighty man.
> Washed his face in a fryin' pan.
> Combed his hair with a wagon wheel.
> Died with a toothache in his heel.
>
> So get out the way, Old Dan Tucker.
> You're too late to stay for supper.
> Supper's over, breakfast's a-cookin'.
> Old Dan Tucker just stands there a-lookin'."

I squeal and laugh and feel like Daddy is the best daddy in these here United States. Then I wake up calling to him. But he ain't there and never will be again.

I still like to think about the fun things we done and the funny stories he used to tell.

We had us a special joke. He'd ask, "How does a cat go?"

I'd say, "Meow."

He'd ask, "How does a dog go?"

I'd say, "Bow wow."

Then he'd ask me with a big grin on his face, "And how does a turtle go?"

He tricked me the first time, but ever time after that, him and me would both say, "Sloooooooooooooow." We'd laugh, and he would give me a big hug.

After we moved into Gramps' house, Daddy added on a bathroom. I'd stand outside and watch him work. Sometimes he let me help. I wore a old jacket that Mama picked up at the Salvation Army so's not to ruin my good one when I played. Daddy and me called it my cementing jacket. I'd hand him tools, and go in the house to get him something to drink when he felt thirsty.

One time he had me fetch a straight, thick stick. I weren't old enough to write, so he put his big hand over my tiny one and helped me scratch *Lydia* in the wet cement. I can still feel his warm, sweaty fingers a-closing over mine. We put my name behind the hole for the toilet. We didn't want Mama and Gran to see it and get all mad. When Daddy put the linoleum down, he cut a rectangle out so's my name wouldn't get covered up. Ever time I cleaned the bathroom after that, I always peeked behind the toilet to see my name. It sure seems strange to have to look behind a toilet to get a good feeling about my daddy.

Gran didn't seem to remember none of them good things when Daddy died. "Good riddance to bad rubbish," she said. "That man was as useless as tits on a boar hog."

Mama told her she shouldn't say such things, even iffen his body weren't able to soak up all the corn liquor he drunk. Daddy could get awful mean when he was all liquored up—as mean as he was good when he wasn't drinking. His whiskers couldn't hide the nasty look on his face when he comed home late, reeking of his time with his drinking buddies, as Gran called them. He smelled sour and fiery.

I'd take one look at him and run to hide under the kitchen table. Then I'd stick my fingers in my ears and close my eyes tight. But it didn't never shut it all out. Never.

Mama and Gran always stood between him and me. Sometimes Daddy hit Mama and Gran and cussed at them like they be snakes. But he was the snake—a mean old copperhead that would strike at anybody that got in the way. Mr. Hinkle read us a scary story called *Dr. Jekyll and Mr. Hyde* for Halloween. Dr. Jekyll was a very good person, but Mr. Hyde acted like a monster. Then you find out they was one and the same man. That man be just like my daddy.

One day Gran stirred apple butter in a giant pot over a fire in the backyard. She said she thought it tasted better when it cooked outside than on a stove. Mama and me sat on the porch, sewing on a quilt. The rocking chair that Daddy built for Mama when they first got married creaked back and forth, back and forth, as she hummed and sewed, hummed and sewed. The smell of the apple butter seeped around us, warming me inside. Daddy should ought to be here, too, I thought, a-playing his jaw harp on one of his good days.

"Mama, why did Daddy have to go and get drunk all the time?" I asked. I bit my lip when it come to me what I done said. Mama always told me, "Iffen you ain't got nothing good to say about someone, don't say nothing." And here I sat, saying something bad about my daddy.

But Mama didn't bat an eye or drop a stitch. "Your daddy didn't drink like that when we first got married, Lydia," she said. "Paul was the handsomest man in the holler, maybe in the whole state of West Virginny, with his coal black hair and hazel eyes." She put down her sewing and looked at the sky like she could see him a-floating in the clouds.

I reached over and touched Mama's yellow hair that fell below her waist. Most times, she wrapped it in a bun. I loved it when she took out the bobby pins and let it hang loose. It remembered me of sunrays. Her blue eyes was the sky. "Mama," I said. "He got hisself the prettiest woman God ever created."

Mama smiled at me and patted my hand. Then she stared at the sky again. "I met him at church," she said. "We both sung in the choir. He had this deep voice that sent shivers right up and down my spine. One Sunday morning, Pastor John asked me to sing a solo. I sang 'We Are Climbing Jacob's Ladder.' After church, your daddy strutted right up to me and told me that he could feel hisself climbing that ladder to Heaven when I sung. Then he asked iffen he could walk me home, just as bold as if he knowed me all his life. On the way to the house, he knelt down and picked me some flowers. 'Here's some lady slippers for my lady,' he told me. His smile and them little yellow flowers lit a candle in my heart."

Mama smiled and got a real faraway look on her face. I think she might have misremembered that I was there. She took a deep breath like she was a-smelling them flowers again.

"When we first got married, your daddy was good and kind to me," she went on, "just like my own papa. But then the war with the Nazis broke out. The day after your daddy heard on the radio that the Japanese attacked Pearl Harbor, he tried to join the army. But they turned him down—said he had flat feet. He told me, 'It ain't much of a man who can't even fight for his country.'"

Mama looked down at her lap and picked some loose threads from the quilt offen her dress. I kept on sewing. I was afeared that iffen I said anything, she would stop talking.

She shook her head. "Your daddy sure didn't act like much of a man after the government turned him down. He stopped going to church. Most of his friends went to fight across the waters. A couple of them didn't never come back. He said he was too ashamed even to go to the funerals. He found hisself some new friends at the honkytonk. Instead of worshipping God, he started worshipping demon liquor."

"Ow!" I said afore I thought. I had stuck my finger with the needle. A drop of blood oozed out.

Mama jumped like a squirrel that done heard a shotgun fired. She handed me her hankie. Then she looked me in the eye. "Lydia, it ain't right for me to tell you all this. It's too heavy a burden for a young'un."

I spit on the hankie and wiped my finger. Then I looked straight on at her. "He's my daddy. I got ever right to know, Mama."

She sighed and got real quiet, like she was a-puzzling it out. Then she looked out the window again and commenced to talk. "I kept thinking maybe iffen I loved him more, he would change," she said, almost whispering. "I tried real, real hard to be a good wife." She sighed again even deeper. "But I learned me a important lesson. You can't never change nobody but yourself. Ain't nothing I could of done to make your daddy happy. He hated hisself too much. And all that hate just kept spilling out on your gran and me."

"When I'm all growed up, Mama, I ain't never going to let a man hit me," I told her.

She turned and looked real hard into my eyes. "Good for you, Lydia. You deserve a man who will treat you like the precious jewel you are."

"Mama," I said. "You deserved better, too."

"You're right, Lydia. All us womenfolk should ought to be treated with respect. I had up and decided never ever to take his meanness no more. Your gran and me had us a plan to leave your daddy after BJ got borned. But the good Lord seen fit to take matters into His own hands."

My mouth got all dry and my insides felt squeezed together just thinking about it. "Where would we of gone, Mama?"

"The Lord would have provided, Lydia."

I had me another question I was afeared to ask. It kept me awake sometimes pondering on it. I figured I might as well spit it out. "Mama, did Daddy go to the bad place after he passed on?"

Mama took both my hands. "Now, Lydia, don't you go a-fretting your pretty head about that none. Do you recollect the story about the thief on the cross asking Jesus to take him to Heaven just afore he died? What did Jesus tell him?"

I had rememorized a lot of Bible verses. Gran saw to that. "Jesus said, 'Today thou shalt be with me in paradise.'"

"That's right, Lydia. I believe your daddy was like that thief, a-waiting until the last minute to do the right thing. I imagine he done hisself some fast praying and getting right with the Almighty when that dirt was a-pouring down on top of him. You're going to see your daddy beyond the Pearly Gates someday. He's going to tell you he's sorry and that he loves you. He'll mean what he says, too." She smiled at me. Then she picked up her sewing and started up rocking again. Real soft-like, Mama sung:

"My heart was distressed 'neath Jehovah's dread frown,
And low in the pit where my sins dragged me down,

I cried to the Lord from the deep miry clay,
Who tenderly brought me out to golden day.

He brought me out of the miry clay.
He set my feet on the Rock to stay.
He puts a song in my soul today,
A song of praise, hallelujah!"

I leaned my head on Mama's shoulder. With Daddy gone, I thought we wouldn't have us no more troubles. The hitting and yelling stopped, but more troubles snuck up on us as quick as fleas to a dog.

4

It's about not judging people.

I felt a troubling today. Me and Uncle William and Aunt Ethel Mae went to their church at the coal camp. It looks a lot like that Samaritan Holiness Church back in Paradise—the one me and my closest kin attended ever Sunday morning and evening, and Wednesday night. They's both pure white on the outside. They's both got a steeple. They's both got wood pews lined up on either side and a coal stove for keeping the church warm in winter. They's both got a cross on the front wall and a place for the preacher to stand up higher than everbody else. A wood sign hangs near the cross and has numbers that can be changed to show attendance and offering. There's a fancy wood box called a pulpit that has a slanted wood top for the big Bible to rest open on during the preaching. The preacher stands behind it and uses it for reading the Word of God. At the front of both of them churches is a altar rail behind a padded step. That's so's people can kneel down to lift up their hearts to God and get saved when the preacher finishes sermonizing.

The only real difference is that the coal camp church has something that looks like a big bathtub behind the pulpit. You have to walk up some stairs to get to it and then down a few stairs to go into the water. They use it for baptizing.

In Paradise, we walk down to the Kanawha River when folks want to get baptized. We sing hymns and always this one as we join up at the river:

> *Shall we gather at the river,*
> *Where bright angel feet have trod,*
> *With its crystal tide forever*
> *Flowing by the throne of God?*
>
> *At the smiling of the river,*
> *Mirror of the Savior's face,*
> *Saints, whom death will never sever,*
> *Lift their songs of saving grace.*
>
> *Yes, we'll gather at the river,*
> *The beautiful, the beautiful river,*
> *Gather with the saints at the river*
> *That flows by the throne of God.*

Gran explained to me and BJ that getting baptized was like taking a bath that would make you feel cleaner than any other. It showed you was trusting God to wash away your sins. After BJ got saved and decided to be baptized, he called it getting dunked. I figure God got a good laugh out of that one.

Gran said, "Them Methodists and Episcopalians only get a sprinkle of holiness on account of only getting a sprinkle of water poured on their heads when they get baptized."

But later Mama told me, "I don't think God cares how much water gets used. He probably cares a lot more about what's in your heart." She also said it was probably best not to tell Gran she said that.

But the biggest difference is the preachers. When Pastor John talks about God he smiles and looks real hopeful. Pastor John says God loved us enough to send his only son to die for us. I figure that must be a whole lot of love. It sure did pain my mama to lose her only son. Pastor John says we's supposed to love each other just like God loves us and not to judge one another. When we sing about God, we all feel like kinfolk.

Seems like the folks here in Confidence have done already judged me afore they even talk to me. Some of them women comed up to Aunt Ethel Mae after my first church service. An old lady with blue hair and crinkled-up hands and face spoke to her. "Dear," she said, "you sure is a saint a-taking in your sister-in-law's daughter after what she done to her own flesh and blood." Then she shook her head and clicked her tongue as she looked down at me.

Aunt Ethel Mae pinched up her face real tight like she done drunk herself some lemonade without a speck of sugar. I expect she thought that made her look like a saint. "Well, we all have to do what we can for our Lord and Savior, don't we?" she said.

The old lady pinched up her face, too. She nodded and patted my aunt's arm. "That's all the good Lord asks of any of us."

I bet Anne of Green Gables would have fierce words for that old lady, something like, "You know a whole bunch more about what the Devil asks of people than the good Lord." That's what Anne would have said. But I didn't say nary a word. I just looked down at the hole in my shoe and thought about how I best cut a piece of cardboard to put in it.

Reverend Sanders, Uncle William's preacher, ain't no better. He seems to think we don't hear too good. He screams and yells while he pounds on the pulpit. It gets real scary when he waves the Bible around like a sword. His face gets all red and sometimes I think he looks like Satan hisself. Sweat pours out of him like he's on fire in the bad place. Today when he started up a-talking about how sinful we be, I wanted to run and hide like I used to when Daddy comed home all liquored up.

The preacher opened his eyes real wide, like he was a-trying to see inside of us. "You can't hide from God!" he shouted. "God knows your every thought." I commenced thinking about God knowing that it's my fault Mama's in jail. My face got real hot and my eyes started to tear up. The preacher saw them tears and lunged toward me like a snake to a baby rabbit. He pointed right at me.

"That's right, little sister!" he screamed. "Know the awful truth of your sin. Confess it to God and be saved!"

I could feel all the eyes of them people boring holes clean through me. Some of them said, "Praise God!" and "Hallelujah." Reverend Sanders got real quiet for the first time. He seemed hopeful that I would spit out some words. But I just sat there, biting my lip and cracking my knuckles and staring down at the floor. Finally, he started up yelling about God again to everbody.

Reverend Sanders don't know nothing nohow about me. I done got saved and baptized at Pastor John's church. I wish the Rapture of the Saints would of come right then and God would of took me clean out of that place. God would pull Mama right through that jail cell like it was water. Her and me would fly up to Heaven together, holding hands and smiling at each other. We'd meet BJ and Gran and even Daddy in the air, just like the song says.

I like to think about Pastor John and them folks at the church in Paradise. But it makes me sort of sad, too, not just for missing them, but on account of recollecting about BJ. One Sunday, it was me what figured out that BJ was sick.

Pastor John—he up and commenced to preach about Jesus talking to crowds of folks. They was all a-pushing and a-shoving, trying to get real close to Jesus. The young'uns tried to move to the front, but the grown-ups shoved them to the back. Pastor John said they acted like a lot of folks today. They think young'uns should be seen and not heard. But he said Jesus didn't never think that way at all. Jesus told all them people, "Let the little children come unto me and forbid them not. For of such is the kingdom of Heaven." That's another Bible verse Gran made me re-memorize.

I looked over at BJ and Mama. Mama sat listening to Pastor John, a-smiling and a-nodding. I heard her say a real soft "Amen." Then I looked back down at BJ, sleeping in her lap. I seen he was wringing wet from sweating like it was the middle of summer. But it was November. I wiped BJ's brow with the sleeve of my sweater. After that I leaned over to kiss him. I knowed right then and there that something weren't right.

"Mama," I whispered. "BJ's sweating bullets."

Mama felt his brow just as everbody got up to sing "Just as I Am." Gran felt him, too. She leaned her head over to the side, like she was a-trying to puzzle it out. But she didn't say nothing. That scared me real bad. Gran always has something to say about everthing.

"And when I kissed him," I whispered some more, "it was like kissing a ham. He tasted all salty."

As it turned out, that meant something awful.

5

It's about Thanksgiving.

Yesterday was Thanksgiving, and I had me a plan to call Mama at that there prison in Ohio. I sure am glad the coal company don't pay folks in scrip no more or they wouldn't have real money to give me when I done chores for them. And I sure wouldn't be able to use scrip in a pay phone.

Uncle William says he's right proud to be a member of the union that helped get rid of scrip. He showed me some pieces that he keeps as souvenirs of the time he felt more like a slave than a wage earner. A miner got paid in scrip for how much coal he dug out of the mine each month. Each mine had its number cut out of the middle of the scrip coins. That way, there weren't no mixing them up with real money.

33

The coal company said they was a-paying miners in scrip on account of it being too hard to keep all that real money on hand for payroll. But Uncle William said they really done it so's they could cheat people. You could only use it at the company store and they could charge whatever they wanted for stuff the miners needed. Iffen a miner didn't mine enough coal to buy food for his family that month, he had to ask for store credit. I think Uncle William and Aunt Ethel Mae went through real hard times when they had to use scrip. I figure that's why Uncle William likes to sing this song about mining sixteen tons of coal just getting a man deeper in debt when he works on his car. He sings real loud when he gets to this part:

> Saint Peter, don't you call me, 'cause I can't go;
> I owe my soul to the company store.

Uncle William says he thinks the company store with their high prices will go out of business soon. I sure hope somebody else puts in a store close by. Some folks around here ain't got a car.

I been saving my money from raking leaves for the neighbors. I even got twenty cents once for watching the foreman's little daughter when him and his wife went to a movie. After I bought my spiral notebook, I had me thirty-seven cents left to call my mama. She asked a policeman to write the phone number down for me after they took her out of the courtroom. I was glad Aunt Ethel Mae didn't see him give it to me, or she would have tooken it. She won't even let me write to Mama. "Now, Lydia, it's just going to make you feel worse," she told me one time. "The best thing is just to put it all out of your mind. We don't want you getting all stirred up over what happened. Ain't that right, William?"

Uncle William had his nose buried in the *Charleston Gazette*. I sat beside him on the couch. I saw him roll his eyes, but he didn't say nothing. I thought it was a good thing that Aunt Ethel Mae didn't see him do that. She just went right on running her mouth, so he didn't have no time to say nothing anyways.

I got this big ache inside from missing Mama. I just wanted to hear her voice on Thanksgiving. My heart felt like it would beat right out of my chest when I thought about it. Mama would be so surprised and happy. I knowed I had to wait till just the right time to sneak out of the house to use the pay phone outside the company store.

I helped Aunt Ethel Mae with the turkey and fixings all morning. Me and Mama and Gran and BJ used to fry up chicken on Thanksgiving. Mama would fix some of her yams, green beans, and potato salad. Gran made pie that tasted like a pumpkin cloud. She told me the secret was to whip up egg whites and fold them in real gentle-like.

We didn't have as much stuff to eat as Aunt Ethel Mae and me cooked up, but we sure had us a lot more fun putting it together. After we got done cooking, we'd hold hands around the table and thank the Lord for the good things that made us glad and the bad things that made us strong.

But it wasn't like that this time. Uncle William kept a-harping at Aunt Ethel Mae while he listened to football on the radio. "When you going to get that meal on the table, woman? A man could starve, you know."

Me and Aunt Ethel Mae worked as fast as we could. Aunt Ethel Mae got all teary-eyed in the kitchen. "I don't know what that man wants from me," she whispered. "I think I should of went out and bought us three of them new-fangled TV dinners from the big grocery store in Charleston. Maybe that would suit him better."

I patted her on the shoulder. But I kept on thinking maybe she should be patting me instead. I was a-swallowing tears of sadness from missing my closest kin. It felt good to let some of them tears come out when I cut up the big store-bought onions for the dressing and green beans.

When we sat us down to eat, Aunt Ethel Mae said the same grace she always says afore we eat. "God is great, God is good. And we thank him for our food. Amen."

"Amen," Uncle William said. "Pass me them taters, Lydia."

I passed him the taters, and the gravy, and the turkey, and the dressing, and the green beans, and the butter, and the yams, and the corn, and the peas, and the biscuits, and the strawberry preserves.

When we all had our plates loaded up and they started

to eat, I bowed my head and prayed my own prayer in my head:

Dear Jesus,

It don't seem like I got much to be glad about. I guess I should be thankful that Uncle William and Aunt Ethel Mae be good enough to take me in, even iffen they don't know much about having young'uns around. And I'm glad my mama is still here in this world with me and that I know she loves me. And thank you for taking good care of BJ and Gran and Daddy up in Heaven. Please tell them hello and that I miss them something fierce.

And, Jesus, you must want me to get real strong, 'cause there sure is a lot of bad stuff right now. You said in the Good Book that you ain't never going to leave me or forsake me. Please stay close and help me get strong enough to find a way to get my mama out of jail.

Amen.

I was afeared that Uncle William and Aunt Ethel Mae might ask me why I was a-sitting there with my eyes closed instead of eating. But when I looked up, I saw they's too busy stuffing their faces to pay me any mind. I ate a few bites and then moved the food around on my plate some with my fork. The few bites I ate felt like rocks in my stomach.

When they got done eating, I jumped up to clear the table so they wouldn't see all the food left on my plate.

Aunt Ethel Mae cut up store-bought pecan and pumpkin pies and set them in front of Uncle William. He took a heaping slice of both. Aunt Ethel Mae took a slice of pumpkin. I was glad she also had pecan pie. I didn't want nobody's pumpkin pie but my gran's. I forced down a few bites and jumped up to clear off the table again.

Uncle William let out a loud belch. "That there cooking was mighty fine, Ethel Mae," he told us. "You, too, Lydia."

My jaw just about dropped open. Aunt Ethel Mae's face lit up like a firecracker on the Fourth of July. "I'm glad you liked it, William," she said, grinning over at him.

I saw my chance. "Why don't the two of you go sit on the couch and listen to the radio," I said. "I'll clean up the kitchen."

Aunt Ethel Mae didn't look at me. Her eyes stayed on Uncle William. "Are you sure you can manage, Lydia?"

"I'm sure. You two go on ahead." I didn't have to tell Uncle William. He already headed toward the couch. Ain't no way he'd do women's work. Aunt Ethel Mae followed him like a puppy. Iffen she had a tail, she would have been a-wagging it off.

I remembered something else to be thankful for as I headed toward the kitchen. I looked up to Heaven and whispered, "Thank you, Jesus, that Uncle William has running water in his house." Then I set about doing all them dishes and pots and pans.

When I finally got everthing washed and dried and put away, I peeked in the living room. Uncle William had his head leaned back, snoring with his mouth drooping open like he was a-catching hisself some flies. Aunt Ethel Mae fell asleep with her head on his lap. The man on the radio still shouted football scores.

I already had my money and the phone number of the jailhouse in my apron pocket. I slipped out the back door. It's been real dry and warm lately, not like wintertime. Most of the leaves still clung on to the trees, all brown and dried up. I felt awful glad the sun warmed up the earth. I outgrowed my winter coat last year, and I been afeared to ask Uncle William for another one. My sweater was a-plenty today.

I got to the phone and looked around. I didn't see nobody. The store was closed. Just like I figured, everbody stayed home a-feasting with their families.

I read the directions on the phone: Remove receiver and deposit five cents. I picked up the receiver and put in a nickel. A lady come on and said, "Happy Thanksgiving. How may I help you?"

She sounded right nice, but I didn't want to tell her I needed to call a jailhouse. "I'd like to call my mama in Ohio, please." I gived her the number.

"All right, darling," she told me. "That will be fifty-five cents for the first three minutes."

I thought I would be able to talk to Mama for a long time. I couldn't talk to her at all. "But I only have thirty-seven cents," I said.

"I'm so sorry, honey, but that's not enough. Is there someone who can give you more money?"

I been holding back them tears real good, but now they started pouring down my face like a waterfall. "No, there ain't no one who will help me," I sputtered out. "My mama's in jail, only she didn't do nothing bad. And I just got to talk to her on account of it's Thanksgiving." I sobbed so hard I don't know how she figured out what I said.

"What's your name, child?" she asked, real gentle-like.

"Lydia."

"Well, Lydia, I wish I could connect you, but I can't. I want you to listen to me, dear. You've saved thirty-seven cents. That's a lot of money. It won't be today, but you keep saving your money. You sound like a smart girl who has been really strong. I know you'll be able to talk to your mother soon. I want you to know, though, that you should plan to save at least a dollar. It will probably take them a while to get your mother to the phone before you can start talking. Now, are you going to be okay?"

"Yes, ma'am," I said, choking out the words, but I weren't too sure.

"All right, Lydia. I'm going to disconnect now. You take good care of yourself. I know your mother would want that."

"Thank you, Operator," I said as I hung up the receiver. Then I sat down on the steps of the store and had myself a good cry.

After all them tears got pushed out of my eyes, I thought about what the operator said—that I sounded strong. Anne of Green Gables stayed real strong when she had to take care of them twins by herself. But I ain't

40

strong. I feel all mushy inside. That operator sounded awful nice, but she don't know nothing about me being so weak. I expect everbody would be ashamed of me, including Mama and that operator, iffen they saw me blubbering like a baby.

Well, as Gran always used to say, there ain't no use crying over spilled milk. I knowed I would have to go back to Uncle William's house afore they missed me. I wiped my eyes real good with the sleeve of my sweater and stood up. "I'm just going to have to make me some more money," I said out loud as I started up walking.

When I got back to the house, I peeked in on my uncle and aunt. They still sat on the couch, sound asleep. I went out on the back porch to set a spell in the creaky swing so's I could think. When we found out about BJ being sick, Gran said God would make us strong. I had plumb misremembered about that.

It seems like a long, long time ago. When we got back from church that Sunday, we laid BJ down for a nap.

He acted all better when he woke up. He weren't sweaty no more either. We sure felt mighty relieved. Mama and Gran put dinner on the table, and I bounced BJ on my knees.

> *"Buttermilk, buttermilk, trot, trot, trot.*
> *Spill the buttermilk, every drop, drop, drop!"*

On the last *drop,* I'd stick my feet out and BJ would slide down my legs. He'd always sparkle with a giggle when I done that. Excepten this time when he giggled, he commenced to coughing real hard. "Mama," I said. "What's wrong with him?"

Mama put her hand on his forehead. "He's a little warm now, but not too bad," she said. "Still, that's a mighty nasty cough." She turned to look at Gran. "Do you think he might have a case of the croup?"

Gran felt his forehead and shook her head, all puzzled-like. "I'm going to fix him up a mustard plaster. Iffen that don't take care of the cough, I think we best get Doc Smythson in the morning."

I put my pinkie close to BJ. He wrapped his little hand around it like he wouldn't never let go. "It's okay, little man," I told him. "You're going to be just fine." But I knowed it was something real bad. Gran didn't never ask to get Doc Smythson. She liked to fix folks up herself. And she liked to fix kinfolks most of all.

The next day, Doc Smythson comed to the cabin and checked BJ over from head to toe. Gran said, "Lydia, tell him what you noticed about BJ at church."

I felt real growed up being asked to talk to the doctor. I told him all about figuring out about BJ being sick. Doc studied me for a time. Then he looked back at BJ. "I think we need to run some tests at the hospital," he said.

So Mama and BJ went back to the hospital in Charleston, and me and Gran stayed home just like we done when Mama birthed him. Doc Smythson had a woman cousin who lived close to the hospital, and Mama stayed there when she wasn't with BJ.

Me and Gran sure did miss them. When they finally got back, Mama and Gran tried to tell me about BJ's sickness. I thought they said he had Sissy Fie Broke It. I figured some lady named Sissy broke his lungs. I used to get afeared that she would sneak into our house some night when we was all asleep and break my lungs, too.

When I got bigger, Doc Smythson talked to me about it one time. He explained that BJ had cystic fibrosis. Ain't no one that broke him. He got borned with it. Doc said BJ would always have that sticky, nasty stuff in his lungs that people get when they have a cold or the flu. And he would catch colds and flu easier than most people and get sicker when he had them. BJ's body wouldn't be able to use all the stuff it needed from food. That's why he stayed real skinny, even though he always ate like he was half starved. Sissy Fie didn't break his lungs, but that sickness sure broke all our hearts.

God made Mama and Gran strong enough to bear their burdens. BJ stayed real strong about bearing his sickness. I wonder why God ain't made me strong.

6

It's about having nothing to do
and my real smart brother.

Aunt Ethel Mae done got herself another sick headache.
Seems like she gets lots of them these days. "Don't let no
light in, Lydia," she whispered to me. I brung her a cold
cloth and closed all the curtains in her room.

When she gets them headaches, she gets real pitiful-
looking, with her face all chalky and her eyes shut tight.
I put a bucket aside her bed in case she throws up. Today's
Saturday and Uncle William didn't have to work at the
coal mine. When she gets like that, he just says a bad
word and takes off somewhere in his car. I ain't sure where
he goes, but my mind does get to wondering about it
sometimes.

I stayed here with Aunt Ethel Mae, waiting for her to

get to feeling better. I wished I could go out for a walk in the woods. I figured I'd play with that big brown dog down the street. He always trots over to see me when I walk to and from school.

I wish I could find me a kindred spirit in Confidence like Anne of Green Gables had. But I ain't got no friends here at all. In Paradise, I went to a one-room school. Kids of all ages studied together. We was more like brothers and sisters than students that just happened to be in the same school. We played together at recess and after school, even if a couple of us had spats from time to time. I had me lots of good friends there.

But in Confidence, the school is bigger. They's three classrooms with three teachers, even though it's one great big room with two thick curtain dividers to section off the classes. I be in the section for fifth and sixth graders with Mr. Hinkle on account of being in the sixth grade. The kids hang out in little groups at recess. I don't know iffen any of them play together after school. I sure ain't invited iffen they do.

Today, when I tried to slip outside to get me some fresh air, Aunt Ethel Mae heared the screen door creaking. "Lydia, is that you?" she said in a real sad and quivery voice. "Could you be a dear and bring me some water?" I drug myself back inside, a-hanging my head like a whupped hound for trying to sneak off and leave her.

I couldn't even turn on the radio. She told me, "Lydia, turn that racket off. It makes me feel like somebody's hitting me on the head with a hammer." To be honest, it makes a body glad for homework. At least then I had me something to do asides sitting real quiet on the couch.

After we found out about BJ being sick, I done most of the taking care of him when I weren't at school. Mama and Gran had work to do, so I didn't mind none. Mama said I was just a little thing, but I could change diapers faster than anybody she'd ever seen. I felt real proud about that. I didn't tell her I changed them fast on account of them smelling something awful.

Mama got small checks from the construction company and the government after Daddy died, but it weren't enough to make ends meet. Gran took in sewing, and Mama took in washing. "We ain't got a lot of money, but we got us each other," Gran liked to say. "That makes us'uns rich!" She was sure right about that. We had ourselves some fun, even when we was a-working real hard.

Gran had this old-timey sewing machine. She got it cheap at the end of World War II when a clothing factory she worked at in Charleston shut down. She would whistle hymns like "Amazing Grace" and "Rock of Ages" in time to her feet pumping the sewing machine, up and down, up and down, up and down. Mama would join in with her mourning-dove voice while she scrubbed clothes on the washboard and pulled them through the wringer. I learned to sing tenor a little, but most of the time I just liked to listen to my mama's voice. I'd pat, pat, pat BJ on the back and bounce, bounce, bounce him on my knees in time to the music. That would help him cough up some of that there sticky, nasty stuff that made it hard for him to breathe.

When Mama finished up with her washing and had hung the clothes on the line to dry, she would get out her dulcimer and sing the melody of some sweet, sweet tunes. Gran would get out her stitching and start to quilting. Then she'd mix her deep alto voice into the songs. I'd get the recorder Daddy made for me afore he passed on, and we'd make us some fine music.

Gran always said, "We can't let our sad rob us of our joy." And we didn't. We sure had us some good times, even with BJ being sick so much. He weren't even a year old when he started dancing to the music and trying his best to sing along. Gran said he learned to talk faster than any baby she ever done saw. And that's a lot of babies! The first word BJ ever said was *sassy-pras*, and he was just three months old. I guess that's 'cause Gran always said she was going to fix herself some sassafras tea. He must of just liked the sound of it.

BJ giggled up at Gran and grinned without a tooth in his head. Him and Gran was alike that way, not having no teeth. "Sassy-pras!" he shrieked.

I thought we would lose Gran right then and there. She fell back in her rocker with her hand covering up her heart. Mama started fanning her with the funeral parlor fan. I runned to get her some cool water from the well.

Gran finally comed back to herself. "Tarnation!" she said. "How did that baby ever spit out that word?"

Mama saw that Gran was okay, so she went over and

picked up BJ. Then she sat with him on the couch. He showed his dimple, smiling up at her. Mama smiled back. "You're just going to have a lot to say to us, ain't you, BJ?"

They locked eyes. "Sassy-pras," he said again, real soft and slow-like.

"That's right, BJ. Sassafras," Mama told him. I think Mama and BJ talked in ways that only they could figure out.

BJ was always right smart. After he learned how to walk, him and me used to go out in the woods. He'd point to every tree, animal, bird, and flower in sight. "What's that, Lyddie?" he'd ask.

"That's a cardinal, BJ."

He'd nod. "That's a carnal," he'd say. "What's that?" He'd point again.

"That's Queen Anne's lace."

"That's keen ann lace. What's that?"

"Them flowers are rhododendrons."

"Road in them ones. What's that?"

"That's a weeping willow."

He stopped walking and looked at me. "How come the tree is crying, Lyddie?"

I didn't know what to say to that. I didn't know what to say to most of them questions BJ asked. And he was full of them.

One day when BJ was three years old, we got supper ready after church. BJ sat on a chair at the table, watching us. "Mama, my Sunday school teacher said God made everthing. Who made God?"

Gran dropped the plate of fried apples she carried, smack-dab on the floor. The plate spun around like a top and them apples went everwhere. "For pity's sake!" she said. "Where does he come up with them things?"

I was afeared BJ might get hisself a whupping for saying something like that.

But Mama just smiled at Gran and sat down beside BJ. "BJ, there's some things that just be way beyond the knowings of even the smartest people in the world. But the smartest people in the world have also figured out that they don't know everthing there is to know. All of us, even the real smart ones, is a-going to have some surprises when we see God face to face. That's going to be a special day, don't you reckon?"

"Yep, Mama, I reckon so." BJ grinned and gave her a hug. Then he skipped out the back door to play.

Something else happened when BJ was three years old that showed us how smart he was.

BJ had to stay in bed for a few days, and he hated it. Gran said most of the time BJ was a busy bee, flying everwhere, never staying long in one place. But when he took sick, Gran said he was the queen bee, ordering all us worker bees to do his bidding. "No, Gran, I'm the king bee," BJ would say.

For sure and certain BJ became the king bee. He'd have me read to him in bed. One day, I started up a new book. It didn't take long afore I felt tired. I wanted to go outside and play jacks with my friends. I figured I would skip over some parts. The first time I tried it, BJ said, "Wait, you skipped some of them words."

I fibbed a little. "No, I didn't," I said.

"Yep. You did so." Then he read me what it was supposed to say.

My eyes got as wide as flapjacks. "BJ, how did you figure out them words?"

"That's easy. It's just talk wrote down."

After I found out BJ could read by hisself, I didn't think I needed to read to him no more. But Mama told me I would have to be his friend as much as his sister when he took sick. I feel bad sometimes when I think that Mama had to make me spend time with BJ. I sure wish I had BJ here with me right now. I'd read to him and play his favorite game, paper covers rock, as much as he wanted.

Mama asked Doc Smythson to call the school board to ask iffen BJ could go to school early on account of being so smart. They sent some man to the house to give him some tests. He said BJ was one of the smartest kids he ever did see. BJ was already reading like a sixth grader, so they let him start school even though it would be two whole *years* until he was six. I'm glad BJ got to go to school afore passing on, even iffen he had to miss a lot of days because of his sickness.

BJ sure did drive them teachers crazy. One time he got sent to the corner for asking one of his questions. "Mrs.

Andrews, I saw two toads mating at the creek on the way to school. They been locked together like that for a couple of days. How long do you think it will be until the female lays her eggs and the male gets offen her back?"

Mrs. Andrews turned red as a ripe tomato and huffed herself up like one of them toads. "Into the corner right now, young man," she said as she grabbed him by the collar and dragged him to the stool. She plopped a dunce cap on top of his head.

BJ was real upset. Gran explained to him that lots of grown-ups don't like to talk about sex, even when it's between animals. "Don't you pay that fuddy-duddy no mind, boy," she said. "You just come to your mama or me iffen you have questions like that." BJ and me called our teacher Mrs. Fuddy-Duddy after that, but just between the two of us.

BJ started scratching his head a couple of days after wearing that dunce cap, and Mama found lice crawling around in his hair. She had to wash his head with some special soap that Doc Smythson gave her. Then her and Gran had to bleach all his sheets. She walked to school with us the next day and told Mrs. Fuddy-Duddy, "I never want you to use a dunce cap on my children again. Iffen you need to punish them, it's fine to send them to the corner, but no dunce cap. Am I understood?"

Mrs. Fuddy-Duddy stared at her, and Mama didn't wait for a answer. BJ made a few more trips to the corner, but he never wore a dunce cap again.

*   *   *

BJ's being smart got him into lots of big fixes. He was five years old when we was woke up in the middle of the night by some loud popping noises coming from the cellar. It sounded like somebody shot off firecrackers. Mama yelled for me and Gran and BJ to get out of the cabin. She picked up the shotgun and headed for the cellar. "Mama, come with us!" I shouted. I just knowed we had ourselves a robber down there.

"No, you all go on now. I'll be all right."

I started to pull BJ toward the door, but he jerked away. "Mama, wait," he said. "Don't go yet. You don't need that gun. I done something real bad."

Mama popped the rifle open and dropped it to her side. She looked hard at BJ. "What did you do, son?"

"Come on. I guess I'd best show you," he said.

We opened the door to the cellar and peeked in. Busted-up jars laid around everwhere. The root beer that me and Mama and Gran had worked so hard to make and store up for the winter covered the ceiling and walls.

Gran shook her head. "That child. I should have knowed" was all she said. Then she went back to bed.

Mama had her hands on her hips. "What happened, BJ?" she asked.

BJ held his hands behind his back and looked down at his shoes. "Mama, I read in one of Lyddie's science books about fermentation. I snuck some raisins in the jars of root beer afore you put the lids on. I had to see iffen the sugar in them would make the root beer ferment. I think it works," he said as he looked around at all them root beer splatters.

Mama put her hand over her mouth and coughed. From where I stood, I could see a grin creeping up around her hand. "That was a very bad thing you done, BJ," Mama said.

BJ still looked at his feet, but he had a hard time keeping his grin down, too. "I'm real sorry, Mama," he said, not sounding sorry at all.

By that time, I thought I would bust. I ran out the back door and let all the laughing pour out.

BJ did feel real sorry when he had to clean out the cellar. He said the worst part of his punishment was having to listen to Gran preach about the evils of demon liquor while he scrubbed the walls.

When Mama and me sat on the porch shucking corn one summer, I asked her how come BJ got borned so smart. "I think the Lord decided that BJ needs to live his life faster than most folks," she said.

I was afeared to ask what she meant by that. But deep in my heart, I'd already done figured it out.

7

It's about how BJ ended up going to Ohio.

SUNDAY, NOVEMBER 29, 1953

I noticed Aunt Ethel Mae didn't leave no meat out to thaw afore we went to church this morning. I asked her iffen she wanted me to pull some leftover turkey out of the freezer. I almost jumped out of my skin on account of the hard look she gived me.

"I don't want to fret about that now, Lydia."

"It ain't no trouble, honest."

"Get on out to the car so's we ain't late for church, you hear me?"

I skedaddled!

On the drive, Aunt Ethel Mae put her hand on Uncle William's shoulder. He shrugged it off.

"William, honey, it just occurred to me that I plumb

54

forgot to lay out some meat to thaw afore we left this morning."

My eyes opened wide! She didn't look at me. Something told me I'd best keep my mouth shut.

Uncle William rolled his eyes and made a grunt that sounded almost like a growl.

"Well, it's a pretty day and all," Aunt Ethel Mae said, "and since we don't have nothing to fix for supper anyways, I thought we might take us a little drive and go out for supper after church." She gived him what I figure she thought was a sweet smile. It looked more like gas pain to me.

Uncle William sighed like he was a-trying to blow out some weight inside him. "Where did you have in mind?"

"If you're sure it's okay, I thought we might go down to Point Pleasant. You know, they've got theirselves such a cute little restaurant that's open on Sunday."

Uncle William mumbled something real low about him thinking God said a man's supposed to rest on Sunday, not go driving around all of creation. At least I think that's what he said. I couldn't hear him too good.

Aunt Ethel Mae's gas pain smile turned into a real smile. She hummed the rest of the way to church.

Uncle William rolled his eyes and didn't say nothing else.

After church, we headed for Point Pleasant. Aunt Ethel Mae jabbered the whole entire way up and back. "I sure wish we could drive to Myrtle Beach right now," she said at one point. "Don't you, William?"

He looked wide-eyed at her and then real quick back at the road. "In the middle of winter? What are you talking about, woman? The ocean would be freezing this time of year."

"I'm just saying, you know, iffen it was warm and all." Then she went on about all them trips they had tooken to Myrtle Beach. Uncle William turned on the radio. He kept turning it up a little at a time. Aunt Ethel Mae just kept on talking a little louder than the music. It got to the point that I wanted to put my fingers in my ears. Uncle William finally gived up and turned off the radio. Aunt Ethel Mae kept on talking, but quieter after that.

I stretched out in the backseat the best I could with keeping my feet on the floor. I sure didn't want to get Uncle William's car seat dirty.

Uncle William didn't seem to like hearing all the talk about Myrtle Beach, but I sure did. I ain't never been to the beach. I wondered what sand felt like when you walked on it in bare feet. Was it scratchy or smooth? Aunt Ethel Mae said the oceans had waves that made a sound that could put you to sleep. I heard the noise the creek makes lots of times when it ripples over rocks. *Does the ocean sound like that?* I wondered. And how did the ocean sand stick together to make a sand castle? I imagined BJ and me running in that water and building castles in that sand. Tears started to burn my eyes, so I tried to imagine Aunt Ethel Mae running in the water in her bathing suit and bathing cap. Pretty soon I had to hold back giggles instead of tears.

When Aunt Ethel Mae stopped talking about the beach and commenced to gossiping about some women at church, I quit listening. Instead, I started thinking about all of them trips we made in Uncle William's car, taking BJ to the hospital in Ohio. BJ was three years old and I was seven when Doc Smythson comed up to the cabin all excited one day. Doc said he found out about a children's hospital that might be able to help BJ. They would treat BJ for free on account of them wanting to study about kids with cystic fibrosis.

We was all happy. Uncle William even said he would take us up there in his car.

It was a long, long drive. We felt all tired and hot and sticky by the time we got to that hospital. Mama sat in the front seat with Uncle William. Gran sat between BJ and me in the back. I felt mighty glad that Aunt Ethel Mae stayed home. We would have been scrunched, and she would have wore our ears out, for sure and certain.

To make the time pass faster, Mama had me and BJ find the alphabet on license plates and figure out who had the most cows on their side. Then we sang for a spell until Uncle William told us to shut our traps so he could pay attention to all them cars on the road.

BJ put his head down on Gran's lap and fell asleep. Gran poured some water from a jar on a clean rag and wiped the sweat offen BJ's face.

I felt too hot to take a nap. We went round and round and round them curvy roads until my stomach started going round and round and round, too. All of a sudden, my breakfast of biscuits and gravy and buttermilk sloshed in my lap and on the car floor.

Uncle William said a bad word as he pulled to the side of the road.

"P.U.!" BJ sat up and leaned his head out of the window. He closed his nose with two fingers and gagged like he might throw up, too. "What did you have to go and do that for, Lyddie?" he asked.

"I'm sorry! I'm sorry! I'm sorry!" I said as tears poured down my cheeks.

"Oh, for goodness' sake," Gran said as she put her arm around me. "It ain't your fault you got a weak stomach. You know what they say. There ain't no use crying over spilt biscuits, gravy, and buttermilk!" She winked at me, and I felt a little better.

Mama laughed, but Uncle William just rolled his eyes. Gran and Mama done the best they could to clean me and the car up with the jar water and rags. Then Gran gived me a piece of hard ginger candy to suck on to settle my stomach.

We stopped at the next gas station to get soap and water from the restroom to finish cleaning up. Gran said the restroom smelled worse than me and the car. I told her I thought it smelled worse than any outhouse I ever used. We learned real fast that we best do our business at home and try to hold it until we got to the hospital. Most times, Uncle William would pull offen the road, and we would find us a tree to hide behind.

We felt all grouchy and plumb tuckered out when we

got to the hospital. A doctor took BJ to check him out real good. Gran waited in the lobby for the doctor to finish up with BJ. Mama had to sign some papers, and me and Uncle William went with her. Mama commenced to read the papers, and she started up asking questions.

The lady behind the desk let out this real long sigh, but she didn't even look up at Mama. She had some other papers she was busy writing on and shuffling around. "You are not going to understand these papers anyway," she said. "If you want your boy to get the help he needs, just sign them."

Uncle William's face got mater red and his teeth clenched tight like he had lockjaw. "Now see here, lady. . . ," he said, looking at her with burning eyes like he wanted to melt her into a puddle. She looked up at him like she dared him to finish what he planned to say.

Mama put her hand on my uncle's arm. "William, we need this hospital to help BJ," she said real soft.

Uncle William snorted, got up out of his chair, and shoved it back under the table so hard I was afeared it might break. "I'll wait outside with Mom," he said as he stomped out of the room.

"Where do I sign?" Mama asked the woman.

Later, Mama said that she made the biggest mistake of her whole entire life when she signed them papers.

8

It's about making Christmas presents.

TUESDAY, DECEMBER 1, 1953

I figured out one thing I can do to keep myself busy. I'm going to start making Aunt Ethel Mae and Uncle William Christmas presents. I ain't got no idea what to make for Mama, stuck in prison as she is. I wonder iffen they even let people celebrate Christmas in jail. Maybe that's part of how they punish them, not letting them get any gifts from family. Iffen them guards in Ohio say it's okay, I hope Uncle William will tell Aunt Ethel Mae to let me send Mama something. I'm afeared Aunt Ethel Mae will commence to crying iffen I ask.

I'm going to embroider Aunt Ethel Mae's initials on her hankies. Maybe I'll add some purple flowers on account of that being her favorite color and all.

One time Uncle William pointed out some big, fuzzy pink dice hanging from a car mirror in the hospital parking lot. He said he sure enough would like to get hisself a pair of them for his car. My jaw about dropped to the ground! I never, ever would of thought he would want hisself a pair of pink dice. But iffen that's what he wants, I figure I can sew him up some.

I'll need six squares for each one of them. I ain't got no fuzzy pink material, but I saw some white muslin in Aunt Ethel Mae's scrap box. I wish Gran or Mama was here to help me mix up some dye. It's been a few years since Gran learned me how to do it. Aunt Ethel Mae growed up too citified to know stuff like this. I hope I recollect how much salt or vinegar to add and how long to soak the material. I think I'm supposed to add salt for berries and vinegar for plants. Or was it the other way around? I'll figure it out, I guess. I sure am glad they's a lot of muslin in them scraps!

Mama and Gran and BJ and me always had fun making gifts for Christmas. We'd whisper to each other about what we was a-making for everbody else. That way we could trade ideas and help each other. But we all kept our lips clamped shut when the gift getter tried to worm it out of us.

BJ was the most ornery about trying to get us to tell them secrets. One time he started up coughing real hard. Mama had went to a ladies' meeting at church to help plan the Christmas party. Gran took herself a little nap in her bedroom.

"BJ, are you okay?" I asked him.

"I'm a-feeling real poorly," he said as he stretched out on the couch.

"Do you want some water? Should I wake up Gran?"

"There is something you can do that might help me feel better." He hacked again.

"What's that?"

"Maybe iffen you told me what Mama and Gran was a-making me for Christmas, I'd be able to think about that instead of about feeling so awful." He looked at me with big, sorrowful, puppy-dog eyes.

"Well, the other night, Gran did tell me what she made you," I said.

Hack, hack.

"I know Gran wants it to be a secret," I went on.

Hack, hack, hack.

"I guess it wouldn't hurt to tell you, seeing as it's just a few more days till Christmas."

Then I saw it. This little, teeny, tiny grin started creeping up the corner of BJ's mouth like a mouse a-climbing up a wall. His eyes didn't look sick no more. They lit up like they was a-giggling!

I put my hands on my hips and stared a grown-up stare at him. "Benjamin James Hawkins!" I told him. "You almost tricked me!"

He busted out laughing. And he didn't hack. Not even once!

* * *

I liked to whittle Christmas presents for BJ. Mama learned me how when I was five. "Your gramps learned me when I was just a little thing, maybe even younger than you," she said. "You must never whittle toward you. Always whittle away from your body."

She showed me how to hold the knife with my thumb on top and fingers curved around the handle. "I like to use cedar because it has such a sweet, comforting smell," she went on. "But the most important thing is to find a piece of wood that speaks to you. Listen to what it tells you it wants to be."

The first thing I whittled was a whimmy diddle. All I had to do was whittle a few notches in a stick. Mama helped me cut a propeller out of a piece of cardboard. The only hard part was to stick a straight pin through the middle of the propeller and into the end of the stick. When I finished, BJ could rub another stick across the notches real fast to make the propeller go around. That was the first Christmas gift I made for BJ out of wood. I felt right proud of that whimmy diddle.

When BJ was four, I decided to whittle him a train for Christmas. Him and me walked to the railroad tracks along the Kanawha River a lot. BJ loved to pretend he was all growed up and riding the train, going on a adventure. He'd make up stories about being a famous doctor, traveling all over America to save sick kids. He took them cures he invented. I was always his faithful companion.

One time, we found a pop bottle on the way. We

stopped at the store to return it and got three cents back. We each bought a stick of licorice for a penny apiece. I told BJ he could have the extra penny. He didn't want to spend it, though. When we got to the tracks, it was almost time for a train to go by. He put the penny on the track. The train came by and squashed it flat. BJ picked it up and held it to the sky. "This is a magic penny," he said. "I'll always keep it with me. When I hold it tight in my hand, it will take me on a train trip, anywhere I want to go."

He did keep that penny with him all the time—in his pocket or under his pillow. Mama said she thought he used his magic penny a lot when he stayed in the hospital.

That's why I knowed BJ would love to have his very own train. Mama thought that sounded like a real hard project, but I just knowed I could do it. Mama said she would make the train whistle.

I commenced to working on the train in August so's I would have plenty of time. I had to whittle on it when BJ stayed at the hospital. That way he wouldn't know about it.

I figured I would make a engine, a car for coal, a passenger car for clothespin people, and a caboose. Mama and Gran gived me good ideas. Uncle William helped, too. Him and me sawed some blocks of wood for the cars. We cut wheels from an old broomstick somebody throwed out in the trash. He let me use some of his wood glue, too.

It took all of us thinking real hard about how to connect them train cars. Gran had the best idea. She said I could use cup hooks. Uncle William bought me some at the hardware store. He paid for them, but I told him I would do some chores for him the next time I went to his house. We had ourselves a deal. On one end of the cars, I screwed in a cup hook that I closed up with a pair of pliers. On the other end, I screwed in a cup hook left open. That way, BJ could put the train together and take it apart any old way.

My very favorite was the caboose. We used beets to make a deep red dye for it. Mama said I could use her black liquid shoe polish for the engine. Grapes made blue dye for the passenger car, and spinach made a good green color for the coal car. Mama thought that train would be the best Christmas present BJ ever did have.

We went to pick up BJ at the hospital on December 23, singing Christmas carols almost the whole trip up there. I kept smiling the entire time, thinking about BJ getting his train on Christmas day. This secret would be hard to keep. Gran and I sat in the waiting area while Mama went up the elevator to get BJ. I kept watching people getting offen the elevator, hoping BJ would come out of them doors.

Finally, I saw him. Mama carried a newspaper and the pillowcase full of his stuff. Nurse Chapel pushed BJ in a wheelchair. BJ's grin covered up his whole entire face, almost. He had a big box on his lap.

"Lyddie! Lyddie!" he shouted. "Come see what I got!"

"Shhh!" Nurse Chapel leaned over and scolded him. "We use quiet voices in a hospital, young man."

"You might, but I don't," BJ said. He didn't even look at her.

I runned over. When I saw the box, it had a picture of a train on it with a big, fancy locomotive.

"Look, Lyddie, look! It runs on electricity!" BJ pulled off the top, and I saw a locomotive, just like the one on the box. There was passenger cars, boxcars, and a caboose. It had lots of track and even a railroad crossing sign. I never ever saw a toy that looked so much like the real thing.

"That's great, BJ," I said. Tears started burning my eyes and quick as I could I blinked them away. BJ was too busy looking at the train to see them tears.

"And I got my picture in the paper, too!" he said. "A real live basketball player gave the train to me. A man took our picture and wrote a story about us. Can Lyddie see the paper, Mama?"

"Not now, BJ," Mama told him. "We need to get on the road." Gran and Mama looked at each other and then at me. I felt my face get hot, and I bit my lip. "Gran and Nurse Chapel will take you to the car, BJ. You can show Gran your picture when you get settled in the backseat. Lydia and I need to stop at the bathroom afore we start back." Gran took the pillowcase and newspaper from Mama.

"How do you know Lyddie has to go to the bathroom, Mama?" BJ asked.

"It's a mother's job to know these things, BJ."

Mama put her hand softly on my shoulder, and we

both turned toward the bathroom. When we got there, the tears started pouring out of my eyes. Mama put her arms around me, and I sobbed into her. "I know. I know this is hard, sweet girl," Mama said as she patted my back.

When I quieted down, Mama ran some water on a paper towel and wiped my face. "Lydia, this doesn't change what you done for your brother."

I looked in the mirror at my puffy face. "Mama," I said, "when we get home, will you let me go in the house first? I want to get the train out from under the Christmas tree and put it in my closet. Maybe some little boy at church will want it."

"No, Lydia. That train stays under the tree for your brother. I think this might turn out different than you think. Let's wait to see what happens Christmas day, okay?"

I told her okay, but I wasn't sure I believed her.

When we got home, Mama told BJ that his new electric train was a Christmas present and belonged underneath the tree. He could play with it on Christmas day. My stomach had a knot in it for the next two days. I kept thinking how embarrassed I would be when BJ opened the gift I had made for him.

The picture in the paper showed the basketball player sitting on the hospital bed with his arm around BJ. BJ's eyes and mouth both grinned. Him and the basketball player held up the train box. The article said that a company donated toys for all them sick kids. Basketball players took time out of their busy schedules to deliver them.

Mama put the picture and story in a old picture frame. She hung it in his bedroom. I felt real thankful that I didn't have to go in there and see it.

On Christmas day, we drank hot sassafras tea and ate cinnamon rolls while we opened our gifts. Mama said, "BJ, you hand out the gifts this year. You already know about your electric train, so why don't you save that for last."

BJ sorted the gifts into piles in front of us. Mama told me to open my gifts first. I forgot about the knot in my stomach. I opened a crinoline Gran sewed for me. (I used to call them stick-out slips when I was little.) Mama made me a new blue dress (my favorite color) with a big white muslin collar and white cuffs on the sleeves. I knowed I would look like them kids in the magazines at the company store, even iffen it was a feed-sack dress. I held the dress up to me and ran to kiss Mama and Gran.

Mama also made me a pine jewelry box lined with felt. Gran gived me a pearl ring that she always wore on the pinkie of her right hand. She said her grandmother gived it to her and now it was time for me to have it. I unwrapped a new whittling knife from Uncle William and Aunt Ethel Mae. BJ had drawed me a picture of me and Mama standing in front of our make-do house. There was a big heart drawed around us. Him and Gran stood off to the side. They had just let go of purple balloons.

Then it was BJ's turn. A knot tightened up in my stomach again. First he unwrapped the train whistle from

Mama. He blew it. *Whooooooo whooooooo!* It sounded just like a real train. Then he opened a Jacob's ladder, two string puzzles, and a marble puzzle that Gran made him. "I don't know why I bother," Gran said. "That boy'll have them puzzles figured out afore day's end." Gran winked at BJ and he winked back.

Mama had also whittled a dancing mountain man for him. A mountain man is real fun. His knees and arms have hinges so's he can fling all around. He has a stick that you hold glued to his back, and he dances on a wood paddle. One end of the paddle is under your leg, and you hold him on the other end like he's onstage. When you tap the paddle with your fingers, he bounces on it and sounds like he's a-clogging his fool head off.

Then BJ found my gift. I had wrapped it up in Sunday funnies Uncle William always saved for us. The knot in my stomach turned into dancing butterflies. I felt tears come up in my eyes. BJ tore off the paper and held up the train. "Wow! A train!" he said. "Lyddie, did you make this for me?"

"Yes," I whispered. I couldn't hold back a few of them tears, and they rolled down my cheeks. "I'm sorry, BJ. I didn't know somebody'd bring you a fancy store-bought one."

BJ giggled. I looked hard at him. "Did you forget we ain't got no electricity, Lyddie? I'm going to have to take it to Uncle William's house to play with it."

I had plumb forgot about that.

BJ took the magic penny from his pocket and put it in his left hand. Then he picked up the train with his right hand and held both of them up to the window so the sun shined on them. "This is my magic train," he said. "When I hold my magic penny, this train will be the one that takes me anywhere I want to go." He put the penny back in his pocket.

Then he commenced to pushing my train around the floor. "See, Lyddie? It don't even need no track. It can go anywhere. It can even flyyyyyyyyy!" he said as he rolled it over the couch and pushed it through the air. He picked up the train whistle with his other hand. Over and over he said, "Clickety clack, clickety clack, going down the track." Then he blew the whistle. *Whoo whoo!*

Me and Mama joined in:

"Clickety-clack, clickety-clack, going down the track.
 Whoo whoo!
Clickety-clack, clickety-clack, going down the track.
 Whoo whoo!"

Gran pulled out a couple of spoons from the silverware drawer and bounced them in her fingers to sound like a train. I runned and got the mountain man and made him dance on my lap. Mama grabbed her dulcimer and started playing a tune. She sang:

"I'm going to get me a ticket, a ticket, a ticket
On engine number seven, on seven, on seven.

70

My gold and silver ticket, it's one way, it's one way, it's
    one way
To take me straight to Heaven, to Heaven, to Heaven."

We had us the best Christmas ever that day. BJ did take the electric train to Uncle William's and they played with it a few times. But it was my train BJ took to the hospital. When I saw him for the last time at the funeral parlor, I laid the train beside him.

9

It's about giving and getting.

Cora Lee walked into Mr. Hinkle's class today with two dresses over her arm. I tried to figure out what in the world she'd need them for. She had this evil grin on her face, the kind where the grin looks happy, but the eyes look mean.

She walked all biggety right up to my desk in front of everbody—excepten Mr. Hinkle. The bell hadn't rung yet, and he stood out on the porch talking to a parent.

"Lydia, my mother said I should give these here dresses to you," Cora Lee said in a real loud voice. "They're out of style now, so I don't wear them. Your mother's in jail, so we decided you probably need them more than anybody else."

My face got real hot. I wanted to do what Anne of Green Gables would do. I bet she would have grabbed them dresses and shoved them in Cora Lee's face. She would have said, "I don't want your dresses. If I washed them fifty times, I'd never get your stinky smell out of them." I didn't say nothing, though. I grabbed me a book out of my desk and started up reading. I pretended like she weren't even there.

Mr. Hinkle walked in the room just then. Cora Lee throwed them dresses on my desk and runned to her seat. I tossed them on the floor.

"Whose clothes are those?" Mr. Hinkle asked, pointing to the heap on the floor.

"I gave those dresses to Lydia, Mr. Hinkle," Cora Lee said with her eyes all sad and her mouth puckered up. "But she won't take them. She threw them down."

"Did Lydia ask you to bring her some dresses?" Mr. Hinkle asked.

"No, but I know she needs them because of her mother being in jail and all."

"Lydia looks fine to me, Cora Lee. She's neat and clean. I think that dress she has on is pretty. I suggest you take those dresses and put them in your locker. Maybe you can take them to your church charity collection."

Cora Lee had to pick up them clothes with everbody watching. I didn't look at her, but I could feel a grin creeping up my lips.

That's just not right what Cora Lee done. Me and Mama had us a talk about giving and getting one time.

Each and ever Christmas, Mama and Gran always made toys for two kids named Betsy and Sylvia that lived down the road from us. They's real poor. Their daddy's been real sick for years and their mama is so sad she ain't up to doing much for her young'uns. When I was in first grade, I seen Betsy stealing and eating food that other kids had throwed in the trash after lunch. I cried when I told Mama about it.

"She didn't steal iffen she took it from the trash. That means it didn't belong to nobody no more. You didn't say nothing to her about it, did you?" Mama asked me as she wiped my tears with her apron.

"No, Mama," I said, all choky.

"Good. That was right kind of you, Lydia. She'd have been real ashamed and embarrassed iffen you had. You was real little when the church took up a collection for us. Do you recollect that?"

"I recollect. Brother Andrew had us stand up in front of everbody. You had BJ in your arms. Me and Gran stood next to you. Brother Andrew said how hard up we was on account of you and BJ being at the hospital in Charleston. He said everbody was real good to help us out and that the Lord would be pleased. Then he counted the money out loud afore handing it to you."

"That's right. How did you feel?"

"I was glad they was a-helping us out, but I also felt kind of sick to my stomach."

"I felt the same way. Pastor John apologized later. He

said he didn't know Brother Andrew would call us up to the front like that."

Mama sat down at the dining room table, and I sat beside her. She covered my hands with hers on the table. "Lydia, the Lord says it's better to give than receive. For most of us, it's also easier. But they be times we all need help," Mama said. "Your gran and me was always used to making do for ourselves. When BJ got sick, we come to realize that we needed help. I ain't sure why it's so hard to ask for it. Pride, I guess. But we come to recollect that God doesn't want us to be alone in this life. He gives us other people to teach us, support us, and comfort us. It ain't right to build a wall around ourselves. Needing help reminds us that we are not sufficient in ourselves, as the Good Book says. That keeps us humble.

"They also be times we can give help to others," Mama went on. "We must be just as humble at those times. Do you remember the story Jesus told about this very thing?"

"The one about them men making sure people watched when they prayed real loud and gived some money to beggars?" I asked.

"That's the one. Jesus said they didn't need a reward from God. They got their reward from making people think they was special and better than everbody else."

"Mama, I don't want Betsy to be hungry."

"I know," Mama said. "I don't want her to be hungry either. Let's make us a plan to help that won't hurt her feelings. How does that sound?"

"That sounds real good, Mama."

So here's what we done. Mama would pack a little something extra in my lunch poke. After I ate my lunch, I'd tell Betsy that I felt full and Mama would get mad at me iffen I wasted food. I asked her iffen she could eat it so's I wouldn't get in no trouble. It weren't no lie. Mama didn't want me to waste food.

Betsy always said yes, she'd be glad to help me out. One time, I asked her why she always saved most of it in her pocket. She told me it was for her little sister. Mama started packing even more food after I told her about that.

At Christmas, me and BJ—when he felt good—got to be secret elves. Gran and Mama always made Betsy's family a couple of quilts for Christmas. On Christmas day, we'd wrap up the presents and food in them quilts. Then, all four of us, we'd sneak over there afore the sun come up. Gran and Mama would hide in the woods. Me and BJ would tiptoe to their house and leave them bundles in front of the door. We would have to keep a hand over our mouths so's the giggles wouldn't come out and wake them up.

It was almost the best part of Christmas. We could picture them opening up them quilts and thinking Santa had brought all them goodies. We kept it a real good secret.

I pray for Betsy and her little sister sometimes. I hope that somebody else will be secret elves for them now that Mama and Gran and BJ and me won't be around at Christmastime.

Mama and Pastor John taught me that giving ain't about showing off. Giving is about getting a real good feeling for reaching out to somebody in a humble way. I feel kind of sad for Cora Lee. She missed out on that real good feeling.

10

It's about what happened to Gran.

Gran left this world two years ago today. Uncle William and Aunt Ethel Mae ain't said nothing about it. Maybe they done forgot. I wish I could go up to the cemetery on Paradise Hill, where Gran be buried, but it's too far a piece to go by Shank's mare.

Sometimes when I first wake up in the morning, I think I hear Gran a-calling to me like she used to: "Lydia, get them lazy bones up out of that bed. The day's a-wasting!"

I'd open one eye up and look at her. The morning sun always sparkled out of Gran's eyes. She'd flash me one of them toothless grins and say, "Up and at 'em. Rise and shine. Get some peppy, grandchild of mine!" Then she'd lean over and give me a kiss right smack-dab on my nose. Her knobby finger would reach up under the cover and give me a tickle under the arm.

I'd start up giggling. "Okay, okay, Gran. I done gived up. I'll get up!"

One time I told her I was too big to get kissed on the nose and tickled. "Oh, so someone's getting too big for her britches, is she?" she said. "We'll just see about that!" She started giving me smoochy kisses all over my face and tickling me with both hands. We both laughed so hard we was a-crying.

"You win! You win!" I said. "I ain't too big! I ain't too big!"

"And you just see to it that you never get too big for some lovin', Miss Smarty-Pants!"

"I promise, Gran," I told her. "Not never."

I sure wish I had me some of her loving right now.

My favorite times was our walks in the woods. From when I was tiny, I remember how Gran would pull her long salt-and-pepper hair into a bun, throw on Gramps' old overalls and boots, and grab the tote she had sewed for carrying herbs. She'd throw in some gardening tools to help her get them out of the ground. Mama would dress me in blue jeans, a shirt, and some rain boots from the Salvation Army thrift store.

I asked Mama why she didn't go with us. She said she wanted me to have the same special time with Gran that she had when she was a little girl. Mama said her part of the walk to the woods was to make us a good lunch. She would tuck sandwiches and pieces of pie or cake wrapped up snug in wax paper in Gran's tote. She'd also tuck in jars of root beer or sassafras tea.

Gran would sling the tote over her shoulder, and off we'd go. I'd stick my hand in her overall pocket to keep close to her while we walked. We'd sing songs. The one I liked best was about a dog named Rattler, I guess on account of wishing I had me a dog. That's why I liked playing after school with that big brown dog that lives down the street. I sure wish he was mine. Anyways, the song me and Gran sang goes like this:

> Rattler was a good old dog, as blind as he could be.
> But every night at suppertime, I believe that dog
>   could see.
>
> Here, Rattler, here! Here, Rattler, here!
> Call old Rattler from the barn. Here, Rattler, here!
>
> Rattler was a friendly dog, even though he was blind.
> He wouldn't hurt a living thing, he was so very kind.
>
> One night I saw a big fat coon climb into a tree.
> I called old Rattler right away, to fetch him down
>   for me.
>
> But Rattler wouldn't fetch for me, because he liked
>   that coon.

I saw them walking paw in paw, later by the light of
the moon.

Here, Rattler, here! Here, Rattler, here!
Call old Rattler from the barn. Here, Rattler, here!

We'd pretend like we was really calling Rattler when we come to that part. Gran and me would put our hands up to our mouths and yell real loud. Sometimes I expected old Rattler to come a-running through the woods.

Gran always said she was taking me to nature's school, and she was my teacher. She learned me real good. I know about good mushrooms and bad toadstools. I know that the milkweed's root can be used in a tea to help you breathe better, but the sap is dangerous for your heart. Heal-all is a mint that can help a sore throat. Dandelion leaves be good to eat in salads or boiled. They help clean the poisons out of your system.

Bittersweet is a devil's weed. They's nice to look at and have pretty berries, but them berries could kill a young'un. Bittersweet also strangles other plants. Gran heard that it was used in witch's brew. And the devil's trinity is three leaves. I stay away from them plants.

Gran also learned me about animals. Sometimes we would stop what we was doing and just listen. Then I'd know we wasn't alone in the woods. We'd hear chipmunks arguing about a acorn. Sometimes we'd follow some tracks and find a deer drinking water from a creek. My favorite

was the birds. We'd see cardinals, whippoorwills, chicka-
dees, bluebirds, and nuthatches. Their whistles and calls
filled up the woods with songs. The woodpeckers' rat-
a-tat-tat kept the beat.

BJ comed with us on the walks when he was old
enough. But sometimes I was glad that BJ was in the hospital so's I could have Gran to myself. I feel like crying just
thinking that I felt that way.

Losing Gran was real hard for me and Mama, but I
think it was hard on BJ most of all. Gran tried her best to
help him get better.

We had to take BJ to the hospital in Ohio more and
more. And he stayed longer and longer each time. Uncle
William finally got so tired of driving back and forth that
he learned Mama how to drive.

When BJ had to go to the hospital, Uncle William
would bring the car to the cabin. Mama would take him
home, and we would drive to Ohio.

Gran hated them doctors at that hospital. Gran's mustard plasters and special tea helped BJ a whole lot more
than them doctors did. Gran worked real hard on that tea.
Me and Mama helped her gather up coltsfoot, horehound,
lungwort, licorice, and pleurisy roots. She added some
honey to it so it would taste sweet. BJ started drinking it
when he was real little, and he drank it like most grown-
ups drink coffee.

But the first time BJ went to the hospital in Ohio
smelling like a mustard plaster, them doctors and nurses

got real perturbed. "You're not going to cure that boy with witchcraft," one of them doctors told Gran.

Gran raised herself up real tall so she could look him square in the eye. "I ain't no witch, you sorry excuse for a no-account doctor," she said. "I'm a God-fearing woman who loves the Lord with her whole heart. I sure ain't seen you doing nothing to make this boy right."

Mama had been real quiet around them doctors until then. "We have had us enough of this foolishness," she said. "I'm taking my son out of here."

Gran smiled at Mama, real proud-like.

"You're not taking Benjamin anywhere," the doctor said. "You signed papers giving us the right to treat him and stating that you would not interfere."

"Well, we're changing our minds," Mama said.

"I'm afraid it's not that easy. Benjamin's care has been paid for by a research study. If you pull him out now, you'll owe us thousands of dollars. I'll do everything in my power to make sure you do not put that child in danger by removing him from this program." He looked at each one of us. "Now, if you don't want to lose your house and land, I strongly suggest that you go back to West Virginia and let us treat this boy properly. When he does come home, there are to be no more homemade remedies. Do I make myself clear?"

Mama and Gran didn't say nothing. They got up and left. I followed behind them.

When we got in the car to drive home, Mama said,

"I guess there ain't nothing we can do. We'll just have to hope and pray that them doctors know what's best for BJ."

Gran looked out the window of the car. "Lord have mercy, what have we got that child into?" she asked. Me and Mama didn't have no answer.

Some of the spitfire went out of Gran that day. When BJ would start up a-coughing, sometimes I would see Gran reach for her herbs. Then she seemed to think twice about it and turned to do something else.

BJ was all bothered by it, too. "Please, Gran, can't I have a cup of your tea?" he asked one day when he was a-coughing. "Maybe just a little?"

"That doctor can go to blazes in a handbag for all I care," Gran said. "Iffen my grandbaby needs some of my tea, he's going to get it."

"I'll help you," Mama said.

"Me, too," I added.

BJ smiled. We all did. BJ drank up his tea and stopped his coughing. We decided the tea and mustard plasters would just have to be our secret. BJ said he would even take a bath in lavender oil afore heading to Ohio iffen he needed to get rid of the mustard plaster smell. That was agreeing to a lot for BJ. He sure didn't want to smell like no girl!

Gran hated that hospital, but she always went with us—excepten one time. We was getting ready to drive to Ohio and bring BJ home for Christmas. "I'm a-feeling a mite poorly today," Gran told Mama and me. "You two go on and pick up BJ. I'll have the house all fixed up for Christmas by the time you get back."

"Are you sure you'll be all right by yourself?" Mama asked.

"Now, don't you fret none about me," Gran said. "William is bringing up a Christmas tree from the woods later on. I'll put the ornaments on the tree and whip up a batch of gingerbread cookies. Then I'll take me a little nap until you get home."

When we got back from the hospital, BJ ran through the door. "Gran, Gran, I'm home! Did you miss me?" Mama and me followed behind. We smelled the gingerbread and pine, and the tree was all decorated with paper ornaments and popcorn strings, just like Gran promised. Then we saw BJ standing in the doorway of Gran's room.

His voice sounded real soft. "Gran?" It was a question this time.

Mama and me runned to the bedroom. When I seen Gran, I stood froze up like a statue, but my heart beat so fast and hard that I heard it inside my ears like a ticking clock.

Mama sat on the bed and stroked Gran's hair. A tear like a tiny drop of dew rolled down Mama's cheek. She pulled the cover up over Gran's head.

BJ runned to a corner of the living room. He curled hisself up in a ball on the floor and sobbed. Mama walked over and sat on the floor beside him. She put her arm around his shoulders. Then she motioned for me to come sit with them. I did, and she put her other arm around my shoulders. By then, I was a-crying, too, like my heart would break, because it did. Even being huddled so close together couldn't fill up the emptiness we felt.

"I know it hurts something fierce," Mama told us. "But your gran had a good, full life. She died in her sleep real peaceful-like. And right now, she's probably up in Heaven filling God's ear about how He can make the place better."

BJ grinned just a little. Then he started up sobbing again. "But, Mama," he said. "She died all alone. No one should die without kin. No one."

"I know, I know," Mama said as she held us in her arms.

11

It's about that last trip to Ohio.

SUNDAY, DECEMBER 6, 1953

"Lydia, come here and look out this window at what your fool of an uncle is doing, and on the Lord's day, too!" Aunt Ethel Mae said.

Uncle William held his jacket tight around him with one hand. He dipped a rag in a bucket of soapy water and washed his car with the other hand.

"Honestly," Aunt Ethel Mae said. "I think he loves that car more than he loves me."

I didn't say nothing, but I figured she might be right about that. Uncle William won that car in a poker game. He said it was the luckiest night of his life. By Aunt Ethel Mae's account, it should have been the night he married her.

Anyways, I still can't believe that he taught Mama to drive his car and let her take it clean up to Ohio. Mama used to tell me that some people say love but don't do love. Other people do love but get all flustered about saying love. She said she'd a heap rather have a doer than a sayer in her life. I guess Uncle William is the doer type.

I felt real glad Mama knowed how to drive, that last time we had to go pick up BJ. Doc Smythson comed by the house early one Saturday morning when BJ was cooped up in the hospital again. He had something to tell Mama about in private. "Lydia, would you hang up the wet clothes on the line for me?" Mama said. "It looks like it's going to be a sunny day."

I got my coat on, grabbed the basket full of clothes Mama had washed out, and went to the back door. I opened and closed it, but I didn't go out. I stood real still and listened hard.

I heard Doc say, "It won't be much longer now. I got a call from his doctor in Ohio. I think you and Lydia should get up to see him if you can."

"They never let Lydia in to see him because she's not thirteen. Will they let us bring him home?" Mama asked.

"No," Doc said. "That was part of the agreement that you signed. He'll have to stay in the hospital until the end. They want to treat him as long as possible. It's important for their study."

I bit my lip, trying to fight the tears. I could tell Mama fought her tears, too.

"That blasted study," Mama said.

"I know," Doc said. "I regret ever telling you about it. I never thought it would turn out like this."

"We always knowed you just tried to help. It ain't your fault," Mama said. "Thank you for coming by. Could you call the company store near William's house and ask them to tell him we need the car—that we've decided to go see BJ? Let me tell him how sick BJ is."

"Of course I will," Doc said. "You all take care now." I heard the door close. I runned into the living room.

"Mama, please. We have to bring BJ home. We can't leave him up there."

"Oh, Lydia," Mama said. "I'm so sorry you heard that. I wanted to be the one to tell you when the time come."

"Mama, we have to bring him home," I said again.

"Lydia, we can't. The doctors be helping him more than we can."

I couldn't give up. "Ain't no medicine going to make him well now, Mama. That's what Doc Smythson said. They can't give him what he needs most. You and me. He has to have his kin. We have to bring him home. We have to." I started up crying.

Mama wrapped her arms around me and stroked my hair. I held her tight. When I finally stopped sobbing, she wiped my face with her apron. Then she looked deep into my eyes and sighed. "Yes, of course we need to bring him home, Lydia. Go get some quilts and a pillow. We're going to bring your brother back with us." She carried the big oxygen tank and mask that BJ had been using afore he went to the hospital that last time. We laid them things beside the door, waiting for Uncle William.

Uncle William dropped off the car. His friend had followed him. They was going fishing. I was real glad Mama didn't have to drive Uncle William home.

Mama didn't tell Uncle William how bad BJ was when he asked iffen he should go, too. She didn't want him to get in no trouble.

We packed up the car as fast as we could after he left. Mama and me made us a plan on the way up. She said them nurses had their hands full on account of a polio epidemic, so it shouldn't be too hard to sneak BJ out. I was going to be the decoy.

When we got to the hospital, Mama sure was right about all them kids being sick. They had beds stacked right up next to each other and even in the halls. Mama had been in so many different rooms to see BJ that she knowed the hospital inside and out. We took some back stairs to get to BJ's ward. Then me and Mama split up.

My job was to keep the nurses on the floor a-staring at me. I went to the far end, away from BJ's ward. I shouted out, "Ain't somebody able to tell me how to find my sister?"

The nurses at the station all looked at me. I saw Mama slip from the stairway at the other end of the hall into BJ's room.

A nurse come running out of one of the rooms. "Be quiet, young lady," she said. "This is a hospital. How old are you?"

"I turned eleven two months ago," I told her. That weren't no fib.

"You are too young to be up here. Where is your mother?"

"I don't know. I got lost. She went to visit my sister. She told me to stay in that room where you wait for people, but I want to see my sister."

"You might be carrying germs that will make these children sicker than they already are. You need to go back to the waiting room and stay until she comes to get you."

"I ain't sick," I said. "I feel just fine." That were almost true. The only sick I felt was a knot in my stomach, worrying about BJ.

The nurse's face got all red. She remembered me of a teapot that needed to let off steam. "Leave right now," she said with her teeth tight together. She put her hands on her hips and stared down at me. Them other nurses stared at me, too.

I felt afeared of them, but I knowed Mama needed more time. "I'm all twisted around," I told them real loud with my fingers crossed behind my back. "Can you all help me find how to get back to that room to wait?"

"Oh, all right," that one nurse said. She took my hand like I was three years old and led me to the elevator. "Can you read the numbers?"

"I ain't got much book learning," I fibbed again with my fingers still crossed. "I expect you'll have to help me."

She sighed and pushed the down button and waited with me for the elevator. When the door opened, she shoved me inside and pushed the button with the number 1 on it. When the elevator door closed, I smiled me a big smile. I had tricked them nurses real good.

I got offen the elevator on the main floor and walked to the parking lot. Mama waved at me from the car. When I got there, Mama had tucked BJ in the backseat, all wrapped up with Gran's sunshine quilt and the oxygen tank hissing air into the mask on his face. When I got in the front seat, BJ pulled up his mask and said real soft and scratchy, "Hey, Lyddie. I hear you're going to win next year's liar's contest at the county fair."

We all laughed, until we saw some nurses run out of the hospital's front door and look around the parking lot. Mama told me to get down on the floor. Then she drove out of there so fast that the tires squealed.

BJ slept the whole way home. He breathed real slow, sucking air from the tank. Mama and I sang hymns to try and make ourselves feel better.

It was getting on toward evening when Mama drove Uncle William's car into our yard. "BJ, we're home," I said. Mama opened the back door and scooped him up with the quilt still wrapped around him. She cradled him to her like a newborn as we walked to the porch, the only noise being BJ's raspy breathing. I stayed a step behind her, carrying that big tank so BJ didn't have to take off his mask.

"It's warm this evening. Let's just stay here, Lydia," Mama said as she sat in the rocking chair, still holding BJ close. I put the oxygen tank beside her. Then I pulled the other rocker up next to her, leaned my head against her shoulder, and reached under the quilt for BJ's hand.

With BJ all wrapped up in Gran's sunshine quilt, we sat in the chairs Daddy made. I felt like we was all there together, a family again—Gran and Daddy with us in spirit. God fired up the sky with blues and pinks and yellows like He was a-telling us we had done the right thing, and He was a-welcoming BJ to Heaven. God kissed us with a soft breeze.

BJ opened his eyes after a time. He pointed toward his mask, and Mama pulled it up a little. "I'm home," he said.

"Yes, baby." Mama stroked his hair back from his face. "We're all where we belong."

BJ smiled and I felt a little squeeze on my hand. He pulled the mask up with his other hand. "I saw Gran, Mama," he said. "She looked all shiny like an angel. She said to tell you it would all work out in the end. I'm going to be with her soon."

"I know, BJ. And you give her a big hug for your sister and me." Mama didn't have no tears in her eyes. She smiled at BJ as she stroked his hair.

I wished I could figure out how she got so strong. I couldn't hold back no more, and I started sobbing into Mama's shoulder. BJ let go of my hand. I looked at him, afeared that he had done gone and left me. I balled my hand up in a fist.

And then I felt BJ lay his flat hand over mine. "Paper covers rock," he whispered. "I win." He grinned at me. He said it with the mask on, but I didn't have no trouble figuring out what he said, even though it sounded like he was talking from the bottom of a well.

I grinned back through my tears. "That's not fair," I told him. "You cheated."

"Sing to me, Lyddie," BJ said. He closed his eyes again.

Somehow I conjured up my voice. I felt shaky at first, but then BJ's favorite hymn carried me to a different place. Mama joined in.

> *"There were ninety and nine that safely lay*
> *In the shelter of the fold.*
> *But one was out on the hills far away,*
> *Far off from the gates of gold.*
> *Away on the mountains wild and bare.*
> *Away from the tender Shepherd's care.*
>
> *'Lord, Thou hast here Thy ninety and nine;*
> *Are they not enough for Thee?'*
> *But the Shepherd made answer: 'This of Mine*
> *Has wandered away from Me.'*
> *Out in the desert He heard its cry,*
> *Sick and helpless and ready to die.*
>
> *All through the mountains, thunder riven*
> *And up from the rocky steep,*
> *There arose a glad cry to the gate of Heaven,*
> *'Rejoice! I have found My sheep!'*
> *And the angels echoed around the throne,*
> *'Rejoice, for the Lord brings back His own!'"*

I ain't sure when BJ's breathing stopped. But when I looked at him after I finished the song, he was gone. He looked real peaceful. The yucky stuff that had made him so sick oozed out of the side of his mouth. My little brother was finally free of that terrible, awful poison. Mama took off the mask. He would never need it again.

I thought I would feel all empty inside when BJ left us, but I declare I heard him whisper in my ear, "Tag, you're it." I knowed right then and there that my BJ was never ever going to be far from me.

"You rest real good," Mama said, and she kissed him on the cheek. She took BJ's magic penny out of his pocket and closed his hand around it.

Later that day, the sheriff took my mama away.

12

It's about solitaire and solitary.

TUESDAY, DECEMBER 8, 1953

Uncle William sat at the table playing solitaire tonight. I figure playing solitaire meant he wanted to be all by hisself for a while. Aunt Ethel Mae didn't see it that way at all. Uncle William had just finished one game and was setting hisself up another one. He laid out seven cards, then six on the next layer. Aunt Ethel Mae got herself another deck of cards out of the bureau drawer and plopped herself down in the chair across from him.

I sat on the couch reading *Gone with the Wind*, this big thick book Mr. Hinkle challenged me to write my book report on. But I could see my aunt and uncle out of the corner of my eye. I decided to walk to the kitchen for a glass of water so's I could find out what Aunt Ethel Mae was up to. I drunk the water real slow afore washing the glass out and setting it in the drain.

Uncle William didn't say nothing. He just gived Aunt Ethel Mae a quick hairy eyeball and laid down five cards on the next layer. She real quick started laying down her cards until she caught up with him. When they both had their cards all laid out, she picked up a jack of hearts from the top of her stack of three cards she had counted out. Then she laid it on a queen of spades on his cards.

"Since we both be playing, we might as well play double solitaire," she said without looking at him. She placed another three of spades on his four of diamonds. Uncle William rolled his eyes, but he picked up a seven of clubs and placed it on her eight of diamonds.

I ain't never heard of triple solitaire, so I knowed I wasn't going to be asked to join them. "I'm headed on to bed," I told them.

"Good night," Aunt Ethel Mae said without looking up from her cards. Uncle William grunted and kept on playing.

I learned *solitary* as a vocabulary word last month. Mr. Hinkle helped us rememorize the meaning by telling us we could think about how we play solitaire alone. *Solitaire* must be one of them fancy foreign words. *Solitaire* sounds all warm and cozy, like reading a book and drinking a cup of hot tea in front of a snapping red and yellow fire when it's snowing outside.

But *solitary* sounds as empty as my heart sometimes.

Solitary is all alone when you wish more than anything to have someone you love hug you and tell you everthing's going to be okay. It ain't easy being solitary. And I know all about being solitary.

After BJ left us, Mama put him in bed and spread out the sunshine quilt on top of him. Then she kissed him on the forehead and smoothed his hair, just like she was a-tucking him in for a good night's sleep.

I was wailing by that time. Mama sat down on the sofa and told me to come to her. I laid down with my head on her lap. She pulled a hankie out from the pocket of her skirt, dabbed her own eyes, and then she handed it to me.

"He's with God and Gran now," Mama said, "and they's all watching over us."

"I don't want him up there with God," I told Mama. "I want him back down here with us."

"I know, baby. I know," she said as she wiped my hair back from my face.

"Iffen God loves us so much, why did He take BJ away? He was just a kid, Mama."

"That's one of them big questions," Mama said. "Lydia, lots of people will tell you things to try to make you feel better. They might say that God just needed another angel. They's going to tell you that it was BJ's time, or that he had already done all he was meant to on this earth."

"That's not true, Mama. BJ was so smart. I just knowed he could have growed up to be the best president these here United States ever had."

"He probably would have," Mama said, nodding. Then she looked out the window like she was a-trying to see BJ in Heaven. "He was a mighty fine boy. I think BJ sensed he was going to die soon, Lydia. A couple of months ago when I was tucking him in for the night, he told me that he thought about folks living and dying. I kissed him on the cheek and told him I hoped he felt better real soon. He looked long into my eyes, and then he says to me,

" 'Mama, last summer I saw a string of ants, and I put a piece of bread from my sandwich on the ground for them. I plopped down on the ground to watch. They marched back and forth, back and forth, trying to carry that hunk of bread down a hole, tiny piece by tiny piece.

" 'Most people is like them ants. They live their whole entire lives dragging bread back and forth. Ain't no one got a lot of time on this earth. Not even them folks that we think of as real, real old. Life's not supposed to be about what we do and how long we live to do it. Life is about who we be. We take what we learn here about being, right up to Heaven. We ain't taking no bread, though.'

"Then he winked at me, Lydia. I told him that must be about the wisest story I ever did hear. BJ told me to be sure and tell you about them ants someday. He hugged me real hard and turned over and went to sleep. I sat there on the side of his bed for a long time, watching him sleep and thinking about what he said."

"Why didn't he tell me about them ants hisself, Mama?"

"I think he knowed you wasn't ready to let go of him."

Tears started up falling faster down my face. "Mama, how come you was ready to let go?"

"Because iffen you love someone and know they's not going to get better—only suffer more and more—they's a point you have to love them enough to tell them it's okay to go. You gived that gift to your brother, Lydia, when you told me to bring him home."

Mama smiled at me. Then her face got real serious. "Lydia, I wish we didn't have to talk about this right now," she said, "but there's some things you need to know."

I sat up and looked at her. My heart beat real fast. Something told me these things was very, very bad. "What is it, Mama?"

"Them doctors will be real angry that I took BJ. I hope they'll think about why I done it and understand. They ain't been much for understanding up to now, though."

"Mama, they'll be real angry at me, too," I said. I felt cold all at once and covered myself with the afghan on the back of the couch. "I told you to go get him."

All of a sudden, there was a knock on the door. Mama put her hands on my shoulders. "Lydia, promise me. No matter what happens, never, ever forget who you be." She went to answer it.

I wasn't sure what she meant, but I nodded. Then she went to answer the door. That's when I started knowing about *solitary*.

13

It's about the rainiest day of my life.

It rained today. Finally. You'd think it would be snowing this time of year, but it's still awful warm for December. This here drought has sure made it hard for farmers. I know they's grateful for this little bit of rain. Aunt Ethel Mae told me she read in the *Gazette* that farmers hope we'll get lots of snow during the winter so's they'll have dark, moist soil for planting in the spring. I been adding that to my prayers.

In geography class, we learned about deserts, where it hardly ever rains. Mr. Hinkle told us some states in this country have deserts. The pictures in my textbook put me to mind of what I always thought Mars would look like. Gran taught me and BJ about the stars and planets when we sat out on the porch of an evening. Me and BJ liked to make up stories about the folks that live there. I wonder iffen people who live in deserts have green skin like the ad for a movie about Mars I seen in front of a picture show one time. I hope West Virginia don't turn into a desert. I don't think I would like having green skin.

After I got home from school today and changed into dry clothes, I pulled back the curtain of the little window beside my bed and watched the rain come down—not raining cats and dogs, as Gran used to say, but soft and gentle, like God let go of the rain from eye droppers. The ground was a thirsty baby, sucking it deep inside as soon as the water touched its lips.

Feeling all alone is like being that thirsty ground. I would drink up the sound of Mama's voice iffen I could only hear it again. I ain't heard her soft, gentle voice speaking to me since the day BJ left us. Doc Smythson knocked on the door that day. He was out of breath after running up the hill from where he parked his jeep. When Mama answered the door, he said, "The hospital called me. They've been trying to reach me for several hours, but I was out on an emergency case. Is BJ with you?"

"Yes, David. He's with us," Mama said. "In his home. With his family. He's in his room."

Dr. Smythson ran into BJ's bedroom. Mama and I followed him. Dr. Smythson sat on the bed beside my brother. "I'm so, so sorry, BJ," he said. Doc rubbed his hand across BJ's forehead and smoothed back his hair, just like I had seen Mama do so many times. I can't remember ever seeing a growed-up man cry afore, but that day I did.

I also can't remember Mama ever calling Doc Smythson by his first name afore, but that day, she did it three times. Mama touched his arm and said, "David, I need your help."

Doc Smythson wiped his eyes and nose with his handkerchief. Then he looked at Mama real gentle-like. "Anything, Sarah, anything at all. The hospital told me they had called the sheriff. Then I called right after. Bob's a good friend of mine. I've told him lots of stories about BJ. Seems the hospital called to inform him that you had taken BJ without permission. The hospital let him know they were trying to get hold of me. Bob decided that this time, the law wasn't going to be something that he was in a hurry to enforce. He's giving me some time with you before he comes."

"The sheriff?" I asked. My heart beat so loud and fast that I was sure they could hear it, too. But they didn't even look at me.

"I understand. Thank you," Mama told him. "I need you to take Lydia to William's house and tell them what's happened. I don't want Lydia to be here when the sheriff arrives. Can you do that for me?"

"Are you sure you'll be okay by yourself?"

"I won't be alone," Mama said. Then she turned to me. "Lydia, I need you to stay with Uncle William and Aunt Ethel Mae for a while."

My eyes got wide. I just lost my brother and now my

mama was sending me away? "Why, Mama? I want to stay here with you," I pleaded. "Please!" I was sobbing so hard I couldn't hardly catch my breath.

Mama put her arms around me and held me tight. I circled my arms around her waist like a rope that held her to me. "Lydia, this is the hardest thing I've ever had to ask you to do," she said. "I'm afeared you're going to have to grow up fast now. Just know that my thoughts will always be touching yours, no matter how much space we have between us. I love you. Don't never forget that." She kissed my forehead. Then she pulled my arms from around her waist, and I moved away from her.

Doc Smythson put a hand on my shoulder. "Come on, Lydia. We need to go now," he said real soft to me. He turned to Mama. "Sarah, I'll be back as soon as I can. My wife's sister is visiting, and I'll bring the two of them with me. We'll make sure everything's done to take good care of BJ. I'll call the sheriff from my house."

"Thank you, David. I'll be here waiting with BJ."

I can't recollect much about those next couple of days. I think Doc Smythson tried to talk to me about Mama and BJ. I don't know iffen I ate or slept. I know I cried until my eyes dried up and swelled almost shut. I can still feel how they stung. Uncle William fixed up their little spare room for me. Aunt Ethel Mae put away the clothes Uncle William must have picked up for me. It was like I woke up on the day of BJ's funeral and an evil magician had waved a wand and set me down in a different place with some furniture and clothes from my old house.

I do recollect the day we buried BJ. I figured it would be like the day Gran died. Just like the sunshine quilt she made for BJ, her day was golden and bright, even iffen it was chilly and dotted with patches of shining snow. I just knowed with the drought that was going on even back last April that God would let it be sunny that day. But that for sure ain't what happened. It was like God and the whole world cried. The rain remembered me of a sheet blowing on a clothesline that finally broke free from its clothespins, whipped back and forth, and then covered the ground.

I couldn't understand why the weather had to be so awful. The day was awful enough without all that rain. Instead of having BJ's funeral in Paradise, we had to have it at Uncle William's church, with that mean Reverend Sanders. Pastor John came, though. He sat in the back. Him and Doc Smythson.

Gran's casket had been open and me and BJ each wrote a note to Gran that we put in beside her. We told her how much we loved her and missed her already. Pastor John told funny and wonderful stories about Gran that made us laugh and cry to think about her. Me and Mama and BJ talked about how good the service was and how it made us feel that Gran was right there with us in our hearts.

But Aunt Ethel Mae said no one should ought to have to look at a child in a casket, so the casket was closed afore people walked into the church. I begged Uncle William to let me see BJ one more time so's I could put his magic train and a letter I wrote next to him.

"Please, Uncle William, you got to let me say good-bye to him. Mama ain't here to do it." I felt like crying again, but my tears was all dried up. Aunt Ethel Mae kept harping at him not to take me, but he told me to get into the car. I ran to get the train and my letter, and then we went to the funeral home in Poca. They was getting ready to take BJ to the church, but Uncle William asked them to let me see my brother.

After making us wait a bit, the funeral director led us to a little room. I walked over to the casket and got a shock. BJ looked like a doll instead of a boy. They had put makeup on him. It was okay for Gran to have makeup on for her burying day. She always wore powder, lipstick, and a little bit of rouge to church. But it sure didn't look right on BJ.

It wasn't my brother lying there. I thought about him laughing up in Heaven about them making him look like a girl. This was just his remembering place. So I put the magic train and letter in with him. To remember. But I knowed his magic train had already carried him away to Heaven.

We walked inside the church later that day, and people kept coming up and saying how sorry they was. I didn't even know most of them. I'm real glad they at least had enough sense not to say nothing about Mama, even though they was probably thinking bad things about her.

Reverend Sanders read the obituary from the paper, and then he started ranting and raving about how people sin and should ought to get theirselves right with the Lord. He never talked none about BJ. He never said how smart and funny he was. He never said how BJ knowed more about God and the Bible and being a Christian than he ever would. To him, my brother was just some words on a piece of paper. To me, he was sunshine and rain all wrapped up in one package. He was my brother, and now he was in a place far away where I could never ever touch him or hear him laugh again.

After Reverend Sanders got done yelling at people, they took my brother out of the church and into a hearse. Uncle William was a pallbearer with some of his friends from work.

Aunt Ethel Mae and me followed the casket down the aisle. When we got to the back of the church, Pastor John stood up and put his arm around my shoulders. "You and your mama are in my thoughts and prayers, Lydia," he said. I looked up at him and tried to smile my thanks.

I could tell he wanted to say more, but Aunt Ethel Mae real quick said, "Lydia, we need to get to the car." She grabbed my arm and pulled me away. She sure had enough time to get hugs and gushy words from some of her friends when we got outside, though. Some people told us they was real sorry they couldn't come to the cemetery, but they didn't think their cars would make it up the hill in the rain.

As it turned out, it was just the hearse, Uncle William's car, and Doc Smythson's jeep that made it up the steep cemetery hill with that curvy dirt road that had turned to mud. Reverend Sanders rode in the front seat of the hearse. Pastor John rode wth Doc Smythson.

We slipped and slided like that mud was ice. When we slid close to the edge of the hill a couple of times, I wondered iffen me and Uncle William and Aunt Ethel Mae would be joining BJ and Gran in Heaven. I looked out the window and saw the bottom of the hill far, far away. Uncle William stopped the car at one point that leveled off some and said, "You and Lydia get out and ride with Doc Smythson and Pastor John in the jeep."

"Ain't no way you're making me a widow," Aunt Ethel Mae said. "I'm staying in the car with you. Iffen you go, I do, too." I figured that meant I was also going with them, whether I wanted to or not. Uncle William rolled his eyes and started the car again. I clenched the door handle, with my heart pounding. Iffen we went over the hill, I was going to try to jump out.

We finally got to the top. Aunt Ethel Mae and me shared a umbrella. I had to stand a lot closer to her than I wanted to. Uncle William didn't use no umbrella. He told Aunt Ethel Mae they was sissified. The rain puddled on the brim of his hat and then dripped onto his shoulders. Doc Smythson and Pastor John both used umbrellas. I guess they decided they would rather be sissified than wet. Reverend Sanders had them people at the cemetery put up a little shelter that was just big enough for him to stand under.

"Ashes to ashes, dust to dust," Reverend Sanders said.

At Gran's funeral, Pastor John threw some dirt on the casket when he said them words. Reverend Sanders didn't throw nothing. I figured he didn't want to get his hands muddy.

I thought about them words—*ashes to ashes, dust to dust.* They made my brother sound like nothing. Like he was and then he wasn't. But I figured them words was just talking about his body. My brother—what was real and important about him—was alive. I knowed that to be true without a shadow of a doubt.

Mama was in jail. BJ, Gran, and Daddy was all in Heaven. I don't know why, on the rainiest day of my life, I felt them all there with me. For one little bit of time standing on that hill in the pouring-down rain, I did not feel solitary.

14

It's about them mean girls again.

Today, right in front of the whole entire class, Mr. Hinkle read a story I wrote about Christmas at the make-do house in Paradise. I could feel my face burning, and I wanted to crawl underneath my desk. When he finished, Mr. Hinkle said, "Lydia, your use of imagery makes me feel as if I'm sitting at the table with you and your family. Well done."

I couldn't help but smile a little when he said that, but I kept my eyes fixed on the ink hole in my desk. My cheeks felt hot when all them kids turned around to stare at me.

Cora Lee, Maggie, and Penny was a-waiting for me when I stepped out the door for recess. "Child killer's daughter is the teacher's pet," Maggie said as she bumped against me.

"Imagery wasn't the only thing you used in your story," Penny told me. She grinned her rotten-tooth smile. "I counted four *ain't*s."

Cora Lee tapped me on the shoulder. When I turned to look at her, she folded her arms. "I have some news for you, stupid," she said. "*Ain't* ain't a word 'cause *ain't* ain't in the dictionary."

She had lit a firecracker inside of me and I shoved her so hard that she fell on her backside.

"How would you know?" I shouted. "You don't even know how to spell *dictionary*, let alone use one."

Cora Lee tried to get up and I pushed her down again. "Mr. Hinkle, Mr. Hinkle," she started to wail. I looked hard at them other two girls, and they stepped back away from me when Mr. Hinkle runned toward us.

"What's going on here?" he asked.

"Lydia shoved me for no reason, Mr. Hinkle," Cora Lee whimpered, sniffing to make him think she was a-crying. He took her hand and pulled her to her feet.

"Is this true, Lydia?"

I didn't say nothing. I just kept on staring with a stone face at Cora Lee.

"Come with me, Lydia," Mr. Hinkle said. "Let's go inside and talk. I'll deal with you three young ladies later."

"But we didn't do nothing, Mr. Hinkle," Cora Lee said, all big-eyed and innocent-like. You could of poured her words on flapjacks, they sounded so sweet.

Mr. Hinkle gave them girls one of his see-right-through-you looks. They just walked away. I knowed I

111

had landed myself in big trouble, but a grin still tried to sneak onto my face when I got to thinking about them girls being put in their place.

When we got inside, me and Mr. Hinkle sat down at the round table in the back of the classroom. "Lydia, your aunt told me your situation before you came here. I've seen those girls teasing you, and I'm sure Cora Lee asked for what she got. I know you must have felt angry when Cora Lee tried to give you those dresses. You must know, too, that I can't condone fighting. Can we figure out a better way for you to handle their teasing in the future?"

I bit my lip and didn't say nothing. I looked down at the floor so I didn't have to see his face.

Mr. Hinkle sighed. "Lydia, I care about you. I know you've had a hard time, but you're very bright. I hope you'll graduate from high school and maybe even go to college someday."

I looked up at him. "Like Anne of Green Gables?" I said.

He smiled. "Why, yes, just like Anne Shirley."

I looked down at the floor again. "Them girls made fun of my story on account of I used *ain't*. I can't figure that out. Maggie and Penny use *ain't* all the time, too."

Mr. Hinkle sighed and shook his head. "Knowing correct grammar and using it are two different things, Lydia," he said. "Those girls were just looking for an excuse to give you a hard time. Almost all of your classmates and the people around here talk the way you do."

He explained to me, "Most people don't understand that mountain dialect is an earlier form of English, dating back hundreds of years. When your ancestors came to America from England, Scotland, and Ireland, the way they spoke English didn't change much from generation to generation as speech did in other areas of the country. The mountains kept West Virginians from having contact with others from different states, where speech patterns were changing."

Mr. Hinkle stopped looking at me and stared out the window. "I love the colorful, well-seasoned dialect of the Appalachian Mountains," he told me. "That's one of the reasons I decided to teach in West Virginia—that, and a very personal reason. I learned as much as I could about West Virginia before I came here."

I wondered about the very personal reason, but I figured he wouldn't want me to ask.

"Lydia, the way you use words echoes Chaucer and Shakespeare," he said. "Did you know Shakespeare loved to write double and even triple negatives? He used multiple negatives to emphasize a point, just as mountain people continue to do today. A poet named Thomas Gray lived in the seventeen hundreds. He wrote a famous poem titled 'Elegy Wrote in a Country Church-yard.' Over the years, somebody decided the title needed fixing and changed *wrote* to *written*."

Mr. Hinkle smiled. "I'm probably making you feel as though you're getting a lecture. I promise I won't give you a test." That made me giggle. "I'm sorry to go on like this," he said. "It's just that it frustrates me to see my students feeling ashamed of their heritage."

"I don't care none, Mr. Hinkle."

"You just gave a good example, Lydia. If you lived in Ohio and said 'I don't care' to a teacher, the teacher would think you meant that you weren't interested in what he had to say."

I could feel my eyes get wide. "I'd like you to tell me more," I said. "I be glad to know them famous people talked like I do."

"I know, Lydia," Mr. Hinkle said. "The way you use 'I don't care' means it doesn't upset you or even that you would be glad to do something. Those were meanings of 'I don't care' in the days of the first Queen Elizabeth. Mountain people are not ignorant. Some of the wisest folks I've ever met are mountaineers. They're merely using a way of speaking that other English-speaking cultures have forgotten."

"You mean it ain't bad to talk like this?" I asked, looking him in the eyes. Me and him both grinned when I said *ain't*. I felt mighty thankful he didn't call us West Virginians hillbillies. We sure ain't, I mean aren't, billy goats.

"No, Lydia. It ain't bad." He winked at me. "It's just different. But you need to learn Standard English, too. Standard English will help you go to college and get you a job anywhere in this country. Will you keep working on that? You can use your beautiful mountain language at home and with friends. At school, I want you to practice Standard English."

114

I told him I would. We made us a plan. He would scratch his ear when I used mountain dialect in class. That would remember me—remind me—to try again.

I hoped Mr. Hinkle would forget about what happened with them girls after all that talk. But he didn't. He told me I would have to stay after school ever day for four days on account of pushing Cora Lee. He had a appointment tomorrow, so I would have to stay after for the first time on Wednesday. He told me he would of made me stay for a full week, but the last day of school afore Christmas break is Monday. I didn't mind so much. It was worth it. I think Anne of Green Gables would of been right proud of me.

15

It's about talking back.

Uncle William and Aunt Ethel Mae was as mad as all get-out that I got myself in trouble and have to stay after school. I couldn't make myself show Mr. Hinkle's note to them yesterday. I thought iffen I gived it to Aunt Ethel Mae this evening while she was busy with her embroidery, she might not pay it too much mind. But she got all watery-eyed. "William, come look what this child has gone and done now," she hollered.

Uncle William stormed in the back door, wearing his heavy coat, his hands all greasy from working on his car. "What are you jabbering on about now, woman?"

I could feel my hands getting all icy cold. I clenched

116

them behind my back and stared at my shoes. I wished I could drop clean through a hole in the floor.

She handed him the note, and I could see him getting greasy smudges on it as he read. Aunt Ethel Mae looked up at me from her chair, her eyes all glassed over with tears. "Lydia, I told you to ignore them girls. This will all go away in time if you pay them no heed."

"But you . . . ," I started.

Uncle William grew to the size of a grizzly bear. His face got all red and blotchy. "Don't you dare sass your aunt!" he yelled. He raised his hand up high.

I figured he would be like Daddy and whup me upside the head. I squinted my eyes real tight and turned my face away from him.

Nothing happened. I finally peered up. Uncle William was a-staring at me, all sad-like, his hand back down at his side. "Lydia, don't disgrace this family," he said, almost in a whisper. "Haven't we had enough of that already?" He headed out the back door to work on his car again. Aunt Ethel Mae turned back to her embroidery, and it was like I wasn't even there no more.

I almost wished Uncle William had hit me instead. I don't think it would of hurt near as much as them words. I walked to my bedroom, laid myself down on my bed, and stared up at the ceiling. My bedroom's so tiny that it can only fit a bed and a little table Uncle William brought from our house in Paradise. All of a sudden, them walls seemed to close in on me, tighter and tighter. I started up panting like a hound in summer. My heart commenced to racing. After a time, I turned over on my stomach and cried so many tears that my pillow was sopped. After I was cried out, I got up to write in this here notebook.

I recollect what Mama used to do when me and BJ got in trouble. She didn't yell. When the weather was pretty outside, sometimes she took us by the hand and said real soft, "Come with me." She'd march us down to the little swinging bridge that stretched across the creek behind our cabin.

"Five times," she might say. We knowed that meant we had to go back and forth across the bridge five times. The first time across was always the hardest. Me and BJ didn't want to walk in step. We'd have to hold real tight to them rope handles. That bridge would slither back and forth like a snake.

But after a while, like magic, we'd start to march, even though we tried not to. The bridge would stop slithering and slide back and forth like Gran's rocking chair. We'd sing jump-rope songs like this one:

> *Teddy bear, teddy bear, turn around.*
> *Teddy bear, teddy bear, touch the ground.*
> *Teddy bear, teddy bear, tie your shoe.*
> *Teddy bear, teddy bear, that will do.*
> *Teddy bear, teddy bear, go upstairs.*
> *Teddy bear, teddy bear, say your prayers.*
> *Teddy bear, teddy bear, turn out the lights.*
> *Teddy bear, teddy bear, say good night.*

It's right tricky to turn around and touch the ground like that teddy bear on a swinging bridge! We'd laugh so hard we forgot all about being mad at each other. When we finally got offen the bridge, we'd still feel like we was a-swinging, and we'd stagger for a time like we had got ourselves ahold of some of that raisin root beer BJ tried to make.

Mama had another trick up her sleeve. Iffen BJ felt too sick for the bridge or it was rainy or dark outside, she brought out a dulcimer wrapped in a special quilt. Now, this weren't just any old dulcimer. Nosiree bob! We believed it was magical! That dulcimer shined reddish brown and gleamed like sassafras tea in a glass mug. And this dulcimer had two fret boards so that two kids could play at the same time.

After Gramps made it, he took Mama and Uncle William to the woods. Gramps gathered pollen from lady slippers, looking around to make sure that no haunts listened in. Then he whispered to Mama and Uncle William that lady slippers really be fairy slippers, and the pollen be fairy dust. He blowed the fairy dust onto the dulcimer. Then he waved his hands over the strings, closed his eyes, and chanted:

> "Fairies high and fairies low,
> Come this day, your powers bestow.
> Bring peace and calm and music sure,
> Tranquil words and melody pure."

I was seven and BJ was three the first time Mama brought it out for us to play. I already knowed all about playing a dulcimer. Mama said it was up to me to learn BJ how to play. So all three of us said the magic chant, and I showed BJ the right way to strum. I learned BJ to play real good. And we never fussed when we strummed the magic dulcimer together. Ever time we finished, my mama always smiled and said the same thing, "My young'uns make such beautiful music together."

I just heard Aunt Ethel Mae and Uncle William outside my bedroom door. "Maybe I should go in and check on her," she whispered.

"Leave her be," Uncle William said.

I should stop writing in this notebook and go to bed. But it sure is going to be hard to get to sleep, fretting about having to stay after school tomorrow.

16

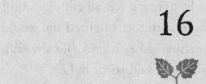

*It's about Maggie pestering me
and having to stay after school.*

WEDNESDAY, DECEMBER 16, 1953

The way of women came on me for the first time today.
I'm glad Mama and Gran done talked to me about it a
long time ago. Gran, with her midwifing and all, said ever
girl should ought to know how God made her body and
what all the parts is for.

Mama said my first time would be real special. That
we would fix us some sassafras tea and figure out something
fun for us two women to do together. But Mama and
Gran ain't here. There ain't no way I'm going to tell Aunt
Ethel Mae what happened. I figure she would probably
just start up crying. I pulled a few rags out of the rag poke,
sneaked some safety pins out of her sewing basket, and
took care of things myself. Then I went on to school.

I'm starting up to feel pulled ever whichaways by them girls in my class. They's as fickle as the sun in January. I'd a heap rather they'd make up their minds to be mean or nice or just leave me alone. Maggie sauntered up to me at recess today whilst I read. My stomach felt all crampy, and I sure didn't need her messing with me. I figured she would bless me out real good for shoving her friend. But she said, "That was right funny what you said to Cora Lee."

I didn't answer.

"Are you deaf or something? What did Mr. Hinkle say to you? I think he is so dreamy, don't you?"

I just shrugged.

"Suit yourself, Miss High and Mighty. You think you're better than the rest of us on account of being the teacher's pet."

I still didn't say nothing. But I did look up from my book and watched her walk off in a huff.

Now first off, Mr. Hinkle's my teacher. You ain't supposed to think of your teacher as dreamy. I feel right certain about that. Second off, I ain't never thought of myself as better than Cora Lee and her two shadows. Never ever. I ain't got nothing. Mama's in jail. I won't never see BJ and Gran and Daddy in this world again. Them girls has everthing, and they don't even know it. I guess I'm going to have to puzzle on this a spell more.

I stayed in my seat after school today, waiting for my punishment. Mr. Hinkle handed me the want ads from his *Charleston Gazette* newspaper. "Here, Lydia," he said. "I want you to read these and write down ideas about

122

what you might want to be when you grow up. You need a dream, and you need to start thinking about your future."

Mr. Hinkle went back to his desk, and I started looking through the want ads. I was trying to find the list of jobs when my eyes fell upon this ad:

FOR SALE
SASSAFRAS ROOT
10¢ A BAG

It all came flooding back—Gran drinking her sassafras tea, BJ's first word, and what Mama told me about us doing something special together. I felt the hole in my heart from missing them grow so big that I thought I would die right then and there. Afore I knew what happened, tears come pouring out of my eyes like a dam done broke. The sobbing caused me to shake all over. I put my head down on the desk, cradled up in my arms, to hide my shame of not being able to stop. I could feel the ink from the wet newspaper sticking to my skin. I shoved the newspaper onto the floor.

Then I felt a hand on my shoulder, real soft-like. I looked up over my arm, and Mr. Hinkle knelt down beside my desk. He pulled a handkerchief out of his pocket and handed it to me. I didn't want to get it all soggy. I reckon he figured that out. He said, "Go on and take it, Lydia. It's a gift. You don't have to give it back."

I took it and wiped my eyes and nose, but I still couldn't stop the crying. The more I tried to pull the tears back in, the louder my sobbing got. Mr. Hinkle kept patting me on the shoulder. "It's okay, Lydia," he said. "Let the tears come. Remember, sometimes it's in our weakness that we are made strong."

So I didn't fight the tears no more. I cried and cried and cried and cried until all the tears had drained out of my heart. Then I felt tireder than I ever been. I think I must of slept a little. When I looked up, Mr. Hinkle had pulled a chair up aside me.

"Lydia, can you tell me what's going on?" he asked.

I already disgraced my uncle and aunt by carrying on with all them tears. I bit my lip and turned my face away from him. I shook my head no.

Mr. Hinkle sighed. "Lydia, I'm here for you if you change your mind. If you don't want to talk about what's troubling you, maybe it would help if we discussed your assignment. Have you found your dream job yet?"

I didn't say nothing.

"Lydia? I need you to talk to me. Can you tell me about your dream?"

Mr. Hinkle is my teacher. I figured I had best answer him and tell the truth. "I only got one dream," I whispered, still not looking at him.

"What is that dream, Lydia?" he asked, his voice also real soft.

"To get my mama out of jail."

"Then when you're ready, Lydia, let's talk about that dream," Mr. Hinkle said. "But now, it's getting late. You

124

had better go on home so your aunt and uncle don't worry."

I think Maggie must have put a hex on me. I looked up, and Mr. Hinkle smiled. I don't reckon I ever paid much attention to his face afore. He's got hazel eyes about the same color as Daddy's. He's right tall and strong like Daddy, too. But Mr. Hinkle ain't never been mean like Daddy—never ever! I'm afeared Mr. Hinkle's what I'm a-going to dream about tonight.

Most of the times when I been walking home from school I get real cold. My coat I brung from Paradise keeps getting tighter and tighter on me. I can't get it buttoned up. I don't want to say nothing to Uncle William and Aunt Ethel Mae about it. I figure I done caused them enough grief as it is. Besides, Gran made this coat for me. I feel like she's walking right along aside me when I wear it.

After making such a scene in front of Mr. Hinkle today, the cold air felt real good on my hot cheeks. It snowed hard, like God was a-covering up the world with a downy blanket. I picked up a handful of snow and held it against my eyes so they wouldn't be so swolled up when Aunt Ethel Mae saw me. The snow smelled clean and fresh, like Mama's hair after she just washed it.

But the heaviness inside weighed me down. I wondered if the sin of what I done to my mama could ever be washed away. It's on account of me that she's in jail. Mr. Hinkle wants me to tell him about my dream to get my mama out of jail, but iffen I tell him, he'll hate me for what I done.

Uncle William and Aunt Ethel Mae told me I ain't never supposed to talk about Mama. They won't let me write her any letters, and I don't know iffen Mama's ever tried to write to me. I know Aunt Ethel Mae would never give me them. She thinks it's best to try to forget about the past so it don't pain me. But how could I ever forget about my mama? And how could I forget what happened at that trial?

Aunt Ethel Mae don't understand that not hearing from my mama just makes the pain worse.

And how will I ever find a way to get my mama out of jail iffen I don't talk to somebody about it?

Everthing is all catawampus.

17

It's about not telling Mr. Hinkle,
and my hope chest.

Thursday, December 17, 1953

The knot in my stomach squeezed tighter and tighter as I thought about having to stay after school again. I don't think I learned much of nothing today. Mathematics and English and history all just got blurred together. Sometimes I looked up and felt surprised that I was in the classroom. All I kept thinking was, *Is Mr. Hinkle going to try to force me to tell him?*

After the bell rang and the rest of them kids ran out of class, I sat in my seat and folded my hands on the desk. Mr. Hinkle walked over and my heart beat faster and my face got hotter with each step he took.

"Lydia," he said as he sat at the desk beside me, "do

you want to finish the conversation we started yesterday? I'd like to help if I can."

It's like all the words I could say fell down a well deep inside of me. I tightened myself up and bit my lower lip so hard it hurt. I kept my hands wound in a ball on my desk and stared down at them. *Please leave me alone,* I kept thinking.

He sighed. "All right, Lydia, it's your choice," he said. "I'm here if you change your mind." He brought me the newspaper. Then he went back to his desk and commenced to grading papers.

I let out my breath. I didn't know I had been holding it in. I picked up the newspaper and started leafing through it to find the want ads. I saw one for Hildegard's Bridal Salon. It showed a drawing of a woman wearing a bridal gown. It made me think of when I saw Mama wearing hers.

It's hard enough that Mama wasn't here for my woman's day, but I can't imagine that she might not be there when I get married or have my babies. Maybe I could wait till she gets out, but I sure don't like the idea of people calling me a old maid. Mama and Daddy married when they was sixteen after Daddy got hisself a job working construction. They had me when they was eighteen.

Ten to fifteen years. That's the sentence the judge laid on my mama. I been thinking about how old I'll be when she gets out of there. I'll be at least twenty-one when she comes home to me. I might be twenty-six.

When I turn sixteen, I figure I'll be old enough to get me a job and get out on my own. Maybe sooner. And I'll go visit Mama in that prison. Nobody will be able to stop me. I know Mr. Hinkle wants me to finish high school and even go to college, but I can't be expecting Uncle William and Aunt Ethel Mae to be taking care of me that long.

When I turned ten years old, Mama gave me a large cedar box with a curved top that her daddy made for her. Gran had lined it with deep-blue velvet. The velvet was crushed and a little faded from the years going by, but that just made it look soft in some places and shiny in the others—real pretty to my eye. Mama told me it was a hope chest for keeping things afore a woman gets married. Gramps surprised her with it for her thirteenth birthday.

Gran walked into the bedroom with us and sat down on the bed. She looked at Mama real puzzled-like and said, "Land sakes, Sarah, why you giving Lydia a hope chest when she's still hoping for a chest on her body?"

"I don't know why," Mama said. "I just feel like she should have it now."

We opened the hope chest together, and there was her wedding dress and the gown she wore on her wedding night. Her and Gran had sewed them. Mama gently lifted the dress that was wrapped in tissue paper. She unwrapped it and held it up to her. "Put it on, Mama, please put it on," I said.

Mama sighed. "Oh, Lydia, I don't know."

"Pleeeeeeease?" I begged, holding my hands together like I was praying.

Mama sighed again. "All right, Lydia. I'll do it for you

and for your birthday." She unzipped her dress and let it slip to the floor. I stood on the bed and held the wedding dress while she shimmied into it.

"Mama, you're beautiful!" I told her with my mouth hanging open. Mama hadn't rolled her hair in a bun yet and it fell around her shoulders, almost like a bridal veil. The sun comed through the window and made her hair shine like gold. I can close my eyes and see that dress just like I'm still seeing it on Mama.

The dress is long sleeved and made from soft white satin. Gran had crocheted a little collar at the neckline. She also crocheted lacy wings that decorated the shoulders. They fell loose at the top of Mama's arms in the back. When I saw them on Mama's dress, I told her, "You look like a angel!"

The waist is long and has a V shape in the front and back. A small satin ruffle puffs below the waist. A line of tiny white buttons like little pearls fall in a straight line from the neck to the waist. Under the ruffle, a skirt of satin with lace organza over the top of it falls long and loose to the ground. Mama and Gran embroidered the organza with the same pattern of leaves and flowers that Gran had used in the collar and shoulder wings.

Mama told me that the long part of the skirt in the back is called the train. I don't know why they call it that, though. When Mama took it off, I felt the satin between my fingers. And then I rubbed the sleeve on my cheek. The dress felt cool and smooth like butter. It smelled of the lavender oil Mama bathed in.

Mama picked up the veil and attached it to her hair with combs. Her and Gran had made it from the same embroidered organza that covered the skirt of the dress. It fell around her like the scarves you see falling around the women's faces in Bible pictures. Then she pulled part of the veil that was plain organza in front of her face.

I asked her iffen she wanted to see how pretty she looked in the mirror, but she didn't say nothing, and she didn't walk to the mirror. She just looked down and started unbuttoning the front of her dress.

I wondered iffen it was hard for her to see them buttons. "How do you see with that veil on when you're walking down the aisle, Mama?" I asked.

"Here, try it on and see for yourself."

She placed it on my head. It was kind of like looking through a screen door. I walked to the mirror on her dresser. I was right surprised. I looked kind of pretty, not like the me I mostly see staring back. I commenced to wondering what my husband would look like and how it would feel to have him kiss me.

"Mercy sakes," Gran said. "You're going to be a looker like your mama when you get a few years on you, young'un."

I ain't never thought of myself that way afore. I felt my cheeks get hot, and I could see in the mirror they was pinking up, even through the veil. "Why do brides wear a veil?" I asked.

"I know the answer to that one," Gran said. "When Moses saw the back of God that time, his face was so shiny

131

that no one could look at him. He had to wear a veil. It's said that a bride's face is so shiny from the love in her heart that no one can look at her."

I had been to several church weddings. "How come her husband can pull it back to kiss her without the shine hurting his eyes?" I asked.

"That's on account of the love in his heart letting him be the only one who can break the spell," Gran said.

"Or maybe the veil's on account of her husband is supposed to be the first one to see her face," Mama said.

I liked Gran's story better. As I was taking off the veil I asked, "Mama, was your face all shiny when you walked down the aisle to meet Daddy?"

She turned her back to me, knelt down, and stroked the velvet in the chest. "I suppose it was, Lydia," she said. She pulled the nightgown from the chest and laid it on the bed.

She started undressing. I helped her take off the wedding dress and zip up her everday one. Then Mama held up the nightgown to her. It looked like the wedding dress excepten it hung down to Mama's ankles and didn't have no lace over the skirt.

Mama wrapped the dress and the nightgown back in tissue paper and placed them in the chest. "I took everthing else out of here, Lydia," she said. "You can wear these for your wedding iffen you want. We can change them some to make them your'n. We'll start sewing some other things for you to put in the chest as you get older."

It was hard to believe that I might wear that beautiful dress someday.

So many things happened after that. BJ started getting sicker. We went to Ohio more often and then Gran died. Mama and me was just too sad and too busy to think of making things for my hope chest. I wish we could of made one thing together—maybe a wedding ring quilt for my bed. Just one thing, like her and Gran done for Mama's wedding.

Uncle William had to leave the hope chest at the make-do house. The bedroom here is too small. I hope everthing is safe back home. Uncle William stops by of a time after work to check on it. He says the house is real dusty but looks okay. He puts out some rat poison to keep them varmints from destroying everthing.

I wish I could go back to the house sometime, but I figure it's best not to ask.

18

It's about telling Mr. Hinkle.

I washed Mr. Hinkle's handkerchief in the sink last night and laid it across my bedpost to dry. This morning, I tucked it inside my bobby sock so as to keep it close to me.

When I got to school, some of the other kids was a-helping Mr. Hinkle decorate a Christmas tree he had put up in the classroom. "Come and join us, Lydia," he called to me.

I picked up one of the paper chains and rubbed my fingers over it. I smelled the pine and recollected the last tree that Gran had fixed up for us. I didn't feel all sad, though. I kept thinking how much Gran loved us, to do that when she felt so poorly. "This is for you, Gran," I whispered as I added my chain to the tree.

Then I heard Gran's voice, real deep inside, say, "Rise and shine, grandchild of mine." I started up thinking of her tickling finger and couldn't help but smile. I sang "Joy to the World" with the rest of them kids.

Mr. Hinkle finally got us all settled into some work. I felt as restless as the tip of a cow's tail, thinking about having to stay after school. Would he ask me about my dream again? The knot in my stomach growed bigger and bigger as the hands on the clock crawled closer to three-fifteen.

Then the rest of the kids left and I was alone with Mr. Hinkle. "Lydia, here is your newspaper," he said. "There are lots of want ads in today's edition." He laid the newspaper on the corner of his desk. Then he picked up a stack of our math papers and commenced to grade them. He didn't so much as look at me.

I felt right perplexed. I got out a piece of paper and a pencil. Then I picked up the newspaper and walked back to my desk. I tried real hard to read them want ads, really and truly I did. But them words was all blurry. Instead of seeing the words, it was like I was looking through a window and seeing my mama trapped in a jail cell on the other side.

The knot inside my stomach kept growing until finally it pushed the words out of my mouth. "It's my fault Mama's in jail," I said in a hoarse whisper.

Mr. Hinkle looked up. "Did you say something, Lydia?"

I pushed the words out again, a little louder this time. "It's my fault Mama's in jail."

Mr. Hinkle got up and pulled his desk chair up close

to me. "Lydia, are you ready to tell me about your dream for your mother now?"

I nodded.

"I know what I read in the newspaper and what others have told me," Mr. Hinkle said. "But I have an idea that there's much more to the story of what happened to your family. I want to know the truth, Lydia. Will you tell me?"

At first, talking about it was hard. But as I started telling Mr. Hinkle about me and Mama and BJ and Gran, it got easier. I even told him about Daddy. One time Mr. Hinkle had to ask me to slow down a little. We smiled together about some of them stunts Gran and BJ pulled.

When I got finished telling Mr. Hinkle about what happened to BJ, he said, "Lydia, you can't blame yourself for telling your mother to go to Ohio to bring BJ home. She made the choice, and it certainly sounds as though it was the right thing to do for your brother. It's not your fault your mother's in jail."

"That's not the only reason why it's my fault," I whispered, the words choking up inside me again.

Mr. Hinkle just looked at me for a spell. Then he looked at his watch. "It's too late to talk more today," he said. "I have to go to a meeting in Charleston, and you need to get home before it gets dark. You've helped me understand so much, Lydia, and I value your confidence in me. We have one more time together after school Monday. If you want, you can tell me about it then."

19

It's about auctions, ice cream,
and that hospital in Ohio.

SATURDAY, DECEMBER 19, 1953

Uncle William and Aunt Ethel Mae went to the auction
tonight. They go almost ever weekend, either on Friday or
Saturday. I had to go with them the first couple of times
after I came to live here. But I started up a-coughing and
a-hacking from all the cigarette smoke. After the second
week, the auctioneer told Uncle William and Aunt Ethel
Mae that they had to leave me at home. I was real glad. All
them people sitting around us kept on giving me dirty
looks like I pestered them on purpose.

Aunt Ethel Mae thought I just pretended on account
of I didn't like auctions. She up and pinched me the first
time. Then she gave me the hairy eyeball when I kept on

a-coughing, and she told me to quiet down. I tried hard to stop, but I couldn't.

"Look at her eyes, woman," Uncle William said. "They's all red. Stop messing with her. She can't help it." Uncle William went outside to smoke on the porch at his house after he saw how much all that auction smoke made it hard for me to breathe. I was real grateful. Aunt Ethel Mae kept on a-smoking and a-smoking in the house. She said I just needed to get used to it.

I felt bad about cigarettes making me cough. Uncle William always planted a cash crop of bacca on Gran's land after Daddy died. He gived Gran and Mama half the money to help us pay bills. The other half he used for hisself and Aunt Ethel Mae. Mama told me once that she thought he let us keep most of it after we found out BJ was sick. But Mama said never ever tell that to Aunt Ethel Mae. I ain't sure we could have gotten by without that money.

Most times when Uncle William and Aunt Ethel Mae go to the auction, I listen to the radio. Gran and Mama and BJ and me always tuned in to the Grand Ole Opry on Saturday nights. I can't listen to it when Aunt Ethel Mae's around on account of that "racket" giving her a headache. She calls it "The Grand Old Uproar." When they's gone, I can sit on the couch a-quilting and a-singing to the music, just like Mama and Gran and BJ and me used to do.

I was glad to have time alone tonight. I finished up my homework, and then I tried to listen to the radio a little, but I had a hard time keeping my mind on it. I finally turned it off. I thought a lot about what Mr. Hinkle told me. Maybe he's right. Maybe what happened to Mama's not my fault. But I still feel a heaviness about it.

Seeing Uncle William and Aunt Ethel Mae come through the door surprised me. They both looked all excited. I ain't never seen Uncle William look that way, excepten maybe when he talks about his car. He grinned and his eyes laughed. They bought theirselves a ice cream maker, the wood kind that you turn with a crank. Uncle William said they got it for a steal on account of no one else wanted to bid on a ice cream maker in the winter. They decided to make some ice cream when they got home—six days afore Christmas!

The auction house is on Tyler Mountain, and it's real close to a store called Van's Never Closed. They stopped there and got rock salt, whipping cream, a bag of ice, and half-and-half. We already had the rest of the stuff we needed.

It was near ten when they got home. We's always in bed by then. But making ice cream is just what we done. Aunt Ethel Mae and me mixed up all the ingredients while Uncle William checked out the machine. We all three talked about the different flavors we could make. I felt right surprised when they said for me to pick the flavor. We had us some peaches we had canned and homemade peach jam, so I said maybe we could make that kind. And maybe we could crumble up some oatmeal cookies to add to it. So we did.

We had to wait thirty minutes for the stuff we mixed

up to cool in the refrigerator afore we put it in the machine. Then we added all the ingredients excepten the cookies in the ice cream maker's tub, and Uncle William added the ice and rock salt around the tub. He cranked and cranked and cranked. He even let me take a turn, and I cranked and cranked and cranked. We added the cookies last. Finally, the ice cream was ready. We each got a spoon and tasted it from the machine. Uncle William said I picked a real good flavor. That was just about the best ice cream he ever done ate. Aunt Ethel Mae said chocolate walnut was still her favorite, but my ice cream flavor tasted mighty fine.

I made some hot coffee for them and some hot tea for me. We sat in front of the coal-burning stove in the living room with our bowls of ice cream.

The three of us talked about all the times we recollected having ice cream from a crank machine. Aunt Ethel Mae sat cuddled up close to Uncle William, and he didn't seem to mind none. I sat on a old cushion on the floor close to the stove. We told about family reunions and all-day-singing-and-eating-on-the-grass days at church. Aunt Ethel Mae didn't even shame me when I talked about Gran and Mama and BJ. I ain't never had that kind of fun with them.

We didn't head to bed until after midnight, and now here I be, writing all this stuff down. I guess that hot tea is keeping me wide awake. I was right surprised but thankful Aunt Ethel Mae said we could skip Sunday school and just go to church so's we can sleep in.

After I curled up under the covers, I thought of something about ice cream that I didn't tell them. One time I asked BJ what his favorite and least favorite things was about the hospital. He said his most favorite things was when his friend Jake stayed at the hospital with him. And also that he got little cardboard containers of ice cream with a wooden spoon almost ever night at supper. His least favorite things was them needles they always poked him with and the way them doctors and nurses always treated him and Jake.

BJ said Jake spent a lot of time at the hospital, too, on account of having something called sickle-cell anemia. Jake told BJ about the pain. He said, "It feels like men with jackhammers bang on my bones and lightning goes down or up my arm. Sometimes it hurts so bad I just jump when it comes." I can't imagine hurting like that.

Most times, BJ and Jake had beds in the back of the ward. BJ said them doctors stood around his bed almost ever day talking about him like he weren't even there. BJ said sometimes he would break wind while they was standing there to teach them a lesson for treating him like that. He said they would go on talking like nothing had happened, but they also crunched up their noses. Most times, BJ acted like nothing had happened neither. Sometimes he would say, "P.U.! Which one of you made that smell?" They just acted like he didn't say nothing.

BJ told me about a time them doctors stood around his bed. "He's from West Virginia, isn't he?" a doctor asked one time. "Perhaps consanguinity is an issue we should investigate. It might benefit our research." Some of them other doctors started laughing until another in the group gave them the evil eye and they shut up real fast.

Them doctors should have investigated how smart BJ was. They had no idea he figured out all the stuff they said about him.

BJ loved words, and he loved the sound of *consanguinity*. He had to tell me that big word about five times afore I could recollect it. BJ recollected it just hearing it that one time. He had to know what it meant. The hospital had a dictionary in the little library they had for them kids. BJ went and looked up that big word. He said it meant them doctors thought Mama and Daddy was related, like first cousins or something.

BJ asked Mama why they would say something like that and laugh about it. Gran heard him and shook her head. "People like to make fun of West Virginians by saying they marry relatives," Mama told BJ. "Generations back, it was a common thing for cousins to marry, and not just in West Virginia. Back then, people didn't know it could cause the children to be more likely to have diseases that are passed on by parents. From what I hear, it still happens with royal folks in other countries. BJ, when people make jokes about it, they be saying West Virginians is ignorant and stupid because their parents married relatives."

BJ's eyes got wide. "Why would they say things like that, Mama? Why do they make fun of people just because of where they be borned? They make fun of Jake, too, just because his skin is darker colored than theirs. I hear them sometimes when they know he's not listening. I can't make any sense of it. I ain't heard none of them making fun of somebody just because their eyes or their hair be a different color."

"It's hard to say, BJ," Mama said. "Do you remember how the chickens we used to have pecked each other?"

"Yep," BJ answered.

"When they peck on another chicken, they be saying, 'I'm better'n you, and don't you forget it.' Them chickens don't see that they's all really the same. They all be chickens—nothing more, nothing less. Some people be like that, too. They pick on other people so's they can think they's more important than they really be. I feel sad for people like that. They must not feel very good about theirselves to put down other folks. They's so busy trying to puff theirselves up that they can't appreciate and learn from people the good Lord puts in their life."

BJ tightened his hands into little fists. "Mama," he said, "I get so mad when they say that stuff. I want to punch them!" He punched the air to make sure we knowed exactly what he meant.

"You could do that, BJ, and it might make you feel better for a while. But you would just be trying to puff yourself up, too."

"What can I do, then, Mama?"

"It can be more fun to laugh at yourself, BJ. You're a right smart boy. You'll figure it out."

The next time BJ went to the hospital, him and Jake did figure it out. BJ asked Mama iffen him and me could

143

buy a piece of licorice when we stopped at a filling station on the way to Ohio. She said okay and gived us each a penny. I ate mine on the trip, but BJ stuck his in his pocket. When I asked him why, he said he had something special to do with it at the hospital.

When he got to come home a few weeks later, BJ told me what him and Jake did. Nurse Chapel used to come in to wake him and Jake up in the mornings. She would stand by BJ's bed and say, "How's our little hillbilly feeling today?" When she finished up with him, she would stand by Jake's bed and say, "How's our little colored boy feeling today?" They hated them wake-up calls. She didn't say nothing like that to them other kids—just "How's Bill feeling?" or "How's Fred this morning?"

BJ and Jake snuck in the janitor's closet and pulled some straws out of a broom. In the playroom, BJ grabbed one of the little tins with eight watercolors that them kids used for painting pictures. BJ always had water and a cup aside his bed, so they didn't have to grab that from nowhere. They had to be real sneaky to get by the nurses and go into the toddler ward. They grabbed a can of baby powder offen the changing table.

None of the kids in the ward liked Nurse Chapel. BJ and Jake told them what they planned to do. Them kids was happy to help. One of them had a little alarm clock he kept on the stand aside his bed. He set the alarm real early so's they could all get up afore Nurse Chapel comed in to wake them.

Then a couple of them kids helped BJ and Jake get

ready. All of them climbed back up in bed and waited. They couldn't hardly hold back the giggles that stuck in their throats.

Nurse Chapel walked in the room, all prim and proper like always. After checking the rest of them kids, she walked back to BJ's and Jake's beds. First she stopped by BJ. "How's our little hillbilly doing today?" she asked as she threw back the cover.

"He's just fine," Jake said. He sat straight up in bed. Nurse Chapel screamed. He had broom straw sticking out from a baseball cap to look like blond hair. His face was covered with baby powder and his two front teeth was coated with black licorice to look like he didn't have no teeth there.

BJ sat up in Jake's bed and said, "Ain't you going to ask how your little colored boy's doing today?" He had painted his face and arms and hands ever color of the rainbow. Nurse Chapel screamed again. All them kids started up laughing.

BJ said Nurse Chapel's face looked like a red balloon about to bust. She grabbed BJ and Jake by the ears and ow, ow, ow, owwed them down to the bathroom to take a bath. BJ said it was worth it. "Aaaaabsoooooolutely!" That's the way he said it. Nurse Chapel never did say nothing about them being a hillbilly or a colored boy again.

I had misremembered about that. I been wishing I could ask Mama what to do about them mean girls. Maybe she done already told me.

20

It's about Aunt Ethel Mae's headaches and Jake.

Aunt Ethel Mae has another one of them headaches today. We stayed home from church on account of her feeling so bad. I weren't too sure iffen maybe she just weren't too tired from staying up so late last night.

But sometimes she looks real sick. I don't think you can fake getting pale and sweaty and throwing up.

I asked Uncle William how come Aunt Ethel Mae didn't see a doctor about all them headaches. He said the coal company don't have the kind of doctor that she needs. When I asked him what kind of doctor she needed, he said, "Never mind."

Uncle William did tell me he once took her to the company doctor. They had to wait several months to get her a appointment. His face got all red and he kept a-shaking his head when he talked about it. "They been taking money out of my paycheck ever month since I started working in the mines to help pay for a company doctor. Excepten when you do get sick, they make you wait until you're well or dead afore you get to see one."

"What did the company doctor say?" I asked.

He rolled his eyes. "That quack only spent a couple minutes listening to your aunt complain. Then he stuck up his hand in front of her face to tell her to shut up and wrote her a prescription for pills."

"Did them pills help?"

"They turned her into a zombie."

I ain't never heard that weird word afore. "What's a zombie?" I asked.

"The living dead."

I got all worried. "Aunt Ethel Mae died and was alive at the same time?"

"No, no. Not like that." Uncle William grinned, and he don't do that often. "I saw this here scary movie at the picture show in Charleston. These dead people comed back alive, but they sure didn't act like their old selves. Their eyes was all glazed over, and they looked at people but didn't really see them. It's like their bodies was alive but their brains wasn't there. That's the way your aunt Ethel Mae was on them pills."

"Are there really and truly zombies?" I asked. I kept thinking about Gran and BJ instead of Aunt Ethel Mae. I wish they would come back alive, but not like that.

Uncle William chuckled deep in his throat like the laugh was swallowed and couldn't get out. Then he looked me in the face and saw I wasn't kidding. "No, Lydia, them zombies was just made up by some guy that had too much time on his hands."

That made me feel better. Then I thought about Aunt Ethel Mae again. "What did you do about them pills?"

"I flushed them down the toilet and filled the bottle with aspirin. After a few days, your aunt said, 'Them pills don't do me no more good than aspirin.' She stopped taking them, so that was the end of that." He looked at me real stern. "You don't need to be telling her about them pills going down the toilet, you hear?"

"I won't." I crossed my heart to promise. I felt real good that Uncle William shared a secret with me, and a little afeared about that there stern look he gave me.

It sure weren't easy for us to get BJ all the doctoring care he needed. We was all so happy that BJ was going to have his medical bills paid for, even iffen we had to take him to Ohio. Mama once told me that we never could have knowed that the cost would be higher than any amount of money.

She told me that Jake's mama said the same thing. Them doctors was busy with their young'uns, so mama and her went to the waiting room to drink coffee and talk. Jake's mama was real glad to get Jake into a white hospital. They moved up to Ohio from Alabama. Her and her husband and Jake's big sister was all crowded into her brother's family's house. She thought Jake would get better care by being part of a study on blood diseases.

Jake's mama also expected Negroes to be treated better north of the Mason-Dixon Line. But them Ohio doctors and nurses looked at skin color just the same. It made her wonder iffen Jake would have been better off in Alabama. They had lots of friends. Most of their family lived close by down South, and some of them had sickle-cell. "At least they would have understood," she told Mama. "The Negro doctors would have treated us with respect and done the best they could to help Jake, even if they didn't have a nice hospital to work in."

As it turned out, that hospital in Ohio didn't do BJ or Jake much good, at least as far as I can tell. After one of his hospital stays, BJ told me Jake wasn't there. He asked Nurse Chapel iffen she knew how Jake was getting on. Nurse Chapel was setting up things on the nightstand aside his bed and didn't even look at him. "He passed away a couple of weeks ago," she said, as iffen she was telling him about the weather outside.

BJ said he got so angry that he felt like he had a hornet's nest inside of him. He hopped offen the bed and stood between Nurse Chapel and the nightstand. "You tell me right now what happened to him!" he yelled.

"Get back in that bed this instant," she said, grabbing his shoulder.

BJ shrugged off her hand and kept a-staring hard at her. "No, you tell me now." He started breathing hard and coughing.

"All right," she said. "Lower your voice. He contracted the flu. Children with sickle-cell anemia have a harder time fighting off illnesses like that. It took his life. Now get back into bed."

BJ said them hornets inside of him started buzzing so loud that he didn't hardly know what he was doing. He kept on shouting, "No, no, no! It's not fair!" Nurse Chapel grabbed his arms, and he started kicking her. He said he barely remembered what happened next. She pushed a button. Some orderlies runned in and held him in bed while Nurse Chapel gave him a shot to calm him down.

Over the next few days, BJ said they forced him to take pills that made him sleep. Maybe that's what Uncle William meant about being a zombie.

When BJ comed home, he talked a lot about Jake. He said them doctors might of tried to fog up his brain, but he weren't never forgetting about his best friend. He knowed he was going to see Jake again someday and they would have a good talk about them doctors and nurses. I didn't say nothing, but I sure didn't like to hear him saying things like that.

I think about Jake's mama sometimes. I wonder iffen she knows what happened to BJ and my mama. It sure seems like they have a lot in common, both of them losing their sons and all.

And I also think about BJ and Jake, causing mischief up there in Heaven, keeping the angels right busy.

21

It's about Mr. Hinkle's betrothed.

MONDAY, DECEMBER 21, 1953

I couldn't sleep last night. I kept thinking about talking to Mr. Hinkle again today and how I still feel like I failed my mama. So I was plumb tuckered out this morning. Afore I went out the door to school, Aunt Ethel Mae called to me. "Lydia, me and William decided you should ought to have yourself a new coat for Christmas. He's going to take us to Charleston tomorrow and drop us off so us girls can shop."

I wanted to hug her, but I didn't know iffen I should. "Thank you, Aunt Ethel Mae," I told her, wanting to bounce up and down but knowing better.

"You're right welcome," she said. "Now get on to school with you."

I forgot all about being wore out as I walked to school.

151

I was excited about going to Charleston and seeing Christmas lights in all them stores. Maybe the Salvation Army band would be playing Christmas carols. I wondered iffen we might get us some hot chocolate at Kresge's 5 and 10. I could feel that warm cup with that candy-bar smell in my hands already. They put whipped cream and a bright red cherry on top. Me and Mama and BJ did that one time. Uncle William dropped us off while he went to do some errands. We didn't have no money for fancy gifts, but BJ said looking at them lights and drinking that hot chocolate was the best gifts ever. I thought so, too.

This time, I was going to get me a brand-spanking-new store-bought coat. I figured out I would like me a blue one. And I could tear my old coat into strips to make a quilt. Then I could still keep Gran close to me.

I had me two knots in my stomach today—one on account of thinking about staying after school and the other on account of being excited about my new coat.

After lunch, someone knocked on the door, and Mr. Hinkle went to answer it. A pretty lady with blond hair and blue-green eyes stood there. She had on this dark green suit and a little hat to match. She looked like some Hollywood movie star and smelled like gardenias. All them boys in my class sat up real straight when they seen her.

"Class," Mr. Hinkle said, "this is Miss Parker. She and I are engaged to be married." Miss Parker held up her left hand and showed us the ring. My heart felt real funny, like it sunk lower inside me. I ain't sure why.

"Miss Parker's family lives in Charleston, and she's

staying with them over the holidays," Mr. Hinkle said. "We met when we were students at Ohio State. She's working in Ohio this year, but she's going to move back to Charleston next summer. We plan to marry in June, and we hope all of you will come." The two of them looked all goofy-eyed at each other. Really and truly goofy-eyed. My own teacher!

"I invited her to spend the afternoon with us. Will you help her feel welcome?" Mr. Hinkle asked.

"Good afternoon, Miss Parker," we all sang. I weren't too sure about her being in our classroom, even iffen she was Mr. Hinkle's betrothed.

"I hope you really do have yourself a good afternoon," Bobby blurted out. His face and ears got all red. We all laughed.

Miss Parker laughed, too. "Why, thank you," she said. "Mr. Hinkle has said such wonderful things about all of you that I couldn't wait to meet you."

Us girls sat up straighter, too, when she said that. I felt real proud that Mr. Hinkle had told her about us. She walked around as we done our work. One time she bent down over me as I wrote a story. "Lydia," she whispered, "I understand you write beautiful stories. Maybe you'll let me read some of them one day." Then she stood up straight and walked to somebody else's desk.

I stared after her. I didn't hear her call nobody else by their name, and I kept trying to puzzle out how come she knowed mine. I got all atwitter thinking about it. Then I got to wondering about staying after school. Was

Mr. Hinkle going to tell me to go on home so he could spend time with Miss Parker? I weren't too sure what to make of it.

When school let out, I didn't know iffen I should get up and go with them other kids or stay behind. Mr. Hinkle must have figured out I was all confused.

"Lydia," he said, "after Miss Parker and I walk the other students outside, we'll be right back."

Maggie stuck her tongue out at me.

"That's enough of that, young lady," Mr. Hinkle said to Maggie. "I'll see you after school when we get back from Christmas vacation."

"Yes, Mr. Hinkle," Maggie said all sticky-sweet-like.

Mr. Hinkle didn't see Maggie smile when she walked out the door, but I sure did. I bet she was real glad she was going to get to stay after school with Mr. Hinkle. And I didn't like it nary one little bit. I ain't sure why it bothered me so much.

I got out a piece of paper and my pencil. I figured with Miss Parker being here, me and Mr. Hinkle wouldn't be talking about my mama. I would have me a boring time reading want ads instead of telling him about that trial. I felt right relieved and right disappointed at the same time.

When Mr. Hinkle and Miss Parker come in the classroom, they each pulled a chair up close to my desk. I could feel my eyes get wide as I pushed back as far as I could into my seat.

Mr. Hinkle got to talking right away. "Lydia, there's

something I didn't tell the rest of the class that you need to know about Julia—I mean, Miss Parker." He looked at her.

"I'm a lawyer, Lydia," Miss Parker said.

"A lawyer?" I said real soft. "But I thought lawyers was all menfolk."

She smiled at me, a real nice, gentle-like smile. "Most of them are, Lydia. But women can achieve their dreams, too, if they're willing to work hard for them."

Mr. Hinkle smiled at her, and then he turned to look at me. "Lydia, when I told Miss Parker what you said about—"

"You told her what I said?" I felt tears filling up my eyes.

"You need to understand that I thought—"

"You told her what I said." I turned my face away from him and shut my eyes. Some tears rolled down my face. I started to reach into my bobby sock. Then I figured out I didn't want Mr. Hinkle's handkerchief touching my face no more.

Miss Parker tried to take my hand. "Lydia, I   "

I pulled my hand away from her. She didn't try to take it again. "All right, Lydia," she said. "I know you're hurt and angry. Sam—your teacher—did the right thing by talking to me. He thought maybe I could help your mother, and he might be right."

I didn't look at them, and I still didn't say nothing. I had done gone and disgraced my uncle and aunt real bad this time. And they planned to take me to Charleston and get me a new coat and everthing. And I already knowed all about lawyers. Ain't no lawyer going to help my mama get out of jail. They just make things a heap worse.

"You have to trust me—both of us, Lydia—if we're going to do anything for your mother," Miss Parker said.

"Lydia, look at me," Mr. Hinkle said. I kept my head turned away and my eyes shut tight. "Look at me!" he said again, a little louder this time. I kept my head down, but I looked up at him. "I know you must feel like I've betrayed you, but I would never intentionally do anything to hurt you. I care about you. You know that, don't you?"

I nodded—just a little. Miss Parker smiled when I done that—just a little.

"Lydia, tell me again what your dream is," Mr. Hinkle said.

I didn't say nothing.

"Tell me your dream," he said louder.

I didn't say nothing. He scooted his chair up closer to me.

"Tell me your dream!" he said as loud as that preacher at Uncle William's church.

"To get my mama out of jail!" I said, real mean-like, looking him right in the eye. Then I started up crying. I reached down and got Mr. Hinkle's handkerchief out of my bobby sock and wiped my face with it. He smiled at me when I done that.

Miss Parker reached over and took my hand again. I didn't pull away this time. Her hand felt all soft, like Mama's. When I kept on crying, she put her arm around

156

me, and I leaned against her shoulder. "I miss Mama so much," I told them.

"This has all been so horrible for you, Lydia. But you've been incredibly strong," Miss Parker told me. "I know you're going to find the strength to do what else needs to be done."

But my mama was in jail because I was so weak. I knowed that her and Mr. Hinkle would be terrible ashamed of me when they found out. And then Mr. Hinkle asked me the question I was most afeared of.

"Lydia, can you tell us what happened at that trial?"

I bit my lip and didn't say nothing. I just shook my head no.

"Lydia, I know this is hard for you," Miss Parker said. "But this is for your mother. You must talk to us."

"But I ain't supposed to," I choked out.

"Who told you that, Lydia?" Mr. Hinkle asked.

"My uncle and aunt. They said they done been disgraced enough already. They said I best forget all about it and get on with my life."

Mr. Hinkle and Miss Parker looked at each another. Miss Parker sighed and shook her head. Mr. Hinkle looked back at me and said, "I've met your aunt and uncle. I know they're good people and want to do what's right for you. The problem is that they've given up hope. You haven't, Lydia—that's why you still carry this dream. And Miss Parker and I haven't given up hope either."

"How come?" I asked.

"Lydia, when I first read about your mother's case in

157

the paper and saw what they had accused her of —" Miss Parker began.

"Child 'dangerment and kidnapping across state lines," I said softly for her. I rememorized them words.

"Yes, Lydia, *child endangerment,* which means causing serious danger to a child, and *kidnapping,* which means taking a child away from the people who are supposed to be taking care of that child. Anyway, if I were BJ's mother, I would have done what your mother did.

"I thought surely she would be acquitted—cleared of the charges," Miss Parker went on. "I was enraged when I found out she had been found guilty. I didn't think there was anything I could do about it, though, until Sam—Mr. Hinkle—told me about talking to you. Lydia, I must know the whole story from you before I can decide if I can help. You need to understand that sometimes the real disgrace is not talking when the truth needs to be told."

I started up crying again. "I know that real good," I said, "'cause that's what I done to my mama."

"Tell us about it, Lydia," Mr. Hinkle said.

I swallowed hard. "We didn't have us no money, so they gived us this lawyer-man for free," I told her. "Uncle William said that man might as well been working for them big-city doctors. Excepten Uncle William used some bad words when he said it."

"Why did your uncle say that?" Miss Parker asked.

"That lawyer-man—he kept on a-looking at his papers like he didn't study up on us at all. He couldn't even

158

recollect Mama and BJ's names without glancing at them sheets."

Miss Parker sighed. "Some of those court-appointed lawyers are excellent and caring. Others border on incompetent, which means they have no clue what they're doing. It sounds as though the one you had did more than sit on the border. He should not be allowed to practice. Lydia, do you know what I mean by *witnesses*?" Miss Parker asked.

"Yes, ma'am. The folks who done spoke for or against my mama. They kept on saying, 'Next witness,' and 'Your witness.'"

"How about *testify* and *giving a testimony*?"

"Folks do that in our church. That's when you tell about something that happened to you that God helped you with."

"That's right. In the courtroom, it means telling the truth about anything that happened to you that might shed some light on whether someone is innocent or guilty of a crime. Who did your mother's lawyer call as witnesses, Lydia?"

I bit my lip and looked down at my shoes. "Me and Uncle William and Aunt Ethel Mae."

"No one else?"

"No, ma'am."

Miss Parker sighed real big. "All right, Lydia. I need you to tell me what happened when you were called to testify."

Big ol' tears started falling out of my eyes.

"You can do this, Lydia," Mr. Hinkle said.

My voice was choky, but I pushed the words out. "When I first went into that big room full of all them people, I felt right afeared. Then I saw my mama sitting up front. I called out to her and started to run over to see her. But Uncle William grabbed me by the shoulder. He told me I couldn't go up there. I had to sit with him and Aunt Ethel Mae."

Miss Parker had some tears in her eyes. "I know, Lydia. They have some rules that are really hard to understand sometimes. What happened next?"

"This man in a big black robe—they called him a judge—he come in and everbody had to stand up. Then this other lawyer—not my mama's lawyer—he got up and said awful things about Mama. He said she murdered my brother, BJ, by taking him out of that hospital. I wanted to stand up and say, 'No she didn't neither!'

"Uncle William looked real mad, too. But he held on to my arm tight, and I knowed I couldn't say nothing. And all Mama's lawyer said—he read it from his paper— was that Mama didn't understand what she was a-doing. But Mama knowed what she was a-doing. She brought BJ home so he could die with his kin."

"I believe you, Lydia," Miss Parker said. "Then what happened?"

"I started up crying real hard, thinking about them telling all them lies about my mama. Uncle William told me to hush up, but I couldn't. Then that judge-man said, 'Somebody get that child out of here.' A woman in a black

160

uniform come over and told me to go with her. I didn't want to, but Uncle William made me."

"Where did she take you, Lydia?"

"We went to this little room with a desk and some chairs. It had a radio in it, and she said I could listen to the radio iffen I wanted. I didn't want to. I asked her iffen I couldn't go back in to be with my mama, but she said no. She said they would take me back in there later."

"Oh, Lydia," Miss Parker said, "you must have been so frightened and confused."

I nodded. "When the lady come back in, she said the hospital's lawyer was done talking to people, and now they was a-taking a break. Then it would be Mama's lawyer's turn, and he'd call me to go up there to speak first. She said iffen I didn't start up crying and making noise no more, I could sit with my uncle again when I got done."

"So then you were called as a witness," Miss Parker said.

"Yes, ma'am. I was afeared to talk in front of all them people, but I knowed I had to speak up for my mama. I wanted to tell them folks how much my mama loved BJ and how them doctors didn't."

"That would have been good for people to know, Lydia," Miss Parker said.

"Some man with a big voice said, 'The defense calls Lydia Jane Hawkins.' My heart beat so fast and hard I thought it might pop right out of my chest. My legs was all shaky like that green Jell-O we got at the cafeteria in

161

BJ's hospital. I weren't too sure I could make it up there. But then Mama turned around and smiled at me. She looked so beautiful, just like always. I wanted to run to her again so I could hug her and smell her hair. But I just smiled back and told my legs to keep walking."

"You were very brave, Lydia," Mr. Hinkle said.

The tears started up again when he said that. I wiped at them with the handkerchief. "So I got up to the front, and the man with the big voice told me to put my left hand on the Bible and hold up my right hand, so I did. But I felt real puzzled. This weren't no church. How come he told me to put my hand on a Bible? And then he said some words that I rememorized when he said them to my uncle and aunt when it was their turn—real scary words."

"What words did he say, Lydia?" Miss Parker asked.

I repeated them words for Miss Parker and Mr. Hinkle. "Do you solemnly swear before almighty God, the seeker of all hearts, to tell the truth, the whole truth, and nothing but the truth, as you will so answer on that last great day?"

Miss Parker and Mr. Hinkle looked at one another. Mr. Hinkle whistled and shook his head. "What did you do, Lydia?"

"I knowed you ain't suppose to swear on the Bible. Gran and Pastor John both taught me that real good. So I pulled my hand away and took a couple of steps back. All the words I planned to say about my mama got choked up inside my throat. That judge-man said, 'The child is obviously not competent to be a witness. Have her step down.'

"When I walked back to my seat, I saw Mama mouth 'I love you, Lydia' and 'It's okay.' I held back crying on account of I didn't want that judge-man to send me back to that room."

"Oh, Lydia," Miss Parker said.

"I know you must be mighty ashamed of me. I should of spoke up for my mama, even iffen God got real mad at me for swearing on that Bible." I started sobbing.

Miss Parker and Mr. Hinkle both patted me on the back, real soft-like. Then Mr. Hinkle left the room. "No, Lydia, we are not ashamed of you," Miss Parker said. "We understand why you did what you did. I'm ashamed of and angry at that lawyer of your mother's. He should have told you what would happen during the trial. Now, I know this is hard, and I know you're tired. But I need to ask you a few more questions. Do you think you can answer them?"

Mr. Hinkle comed back in with a cup of water. I nodded to Miss Parker, and then I drunk the water.

"What happened when your uncle and aunt were called as witnesses?" Miss Parker asked.

"Uncle William got all mad when them lawyers started asking him questions. That judge-man kept on threatening to throw him in jail iffen he didn't settle down. And Aunt Ethel Mae pretty much just cried when her turn comed up.

"When they finished up with Uncle William and Aunt Ethel Mae, them lawyers talked to the people that would decide what happened to Mama. That judge-man told us all to go out while them people figured it out. When he called us back, them folks had up and decided the wrong thing. They believed Mama killed BJ, and Mama had to go to prison. I cried and tried to run to Mama, but Uncle William grabbed me. 'You can't, Lydia,' he said without looking at me. Them guards took Mama away. She just hung her head. Me and Aunt Ethel Mae held on to each other and cried. Even Uncle William wiped his eyes."

None of us said nothing for a time. Then Miss Parker spoke. "Lydia, there are a couple of other things I need to know. Did your doctor or pastor from West Virginia testify?"

"No, ma'am."

"Do you remember telling Sam about the lady who told your mother not to read those papers before she signed them?"

"Yes, ma'am."

"Do you remember what she looked like? Do you think you could pick her out of a group of people?"

"Yes, ma'am. I rememorize things real good."

Mr. Hinkle looked at her. "That's true, Julia. Lydia has an extraordinary memory."

"Yes, I can tell from what's she's told us already. It's quite remarkable."

I smiled real big when they said them things about me. Miss Parker smiled. "That's excellent Lydia. Now, I understand your uncle was also in the room when that woman said not to read the papers. Is that true?"

"Yes, ma'am. He got in a big huff about it."

"Lydia," Miss Parker said. "I think I can help your mother, but I'll need you to be a witness again. Can you do that?"

I kept thinking about what happened the last time. I felt real dizzy. "I don't know."

"We realize it will be difficult," Mr. Hinkle said. "But Miss Parker and I believe you can do this."

"But that judge said I wasn't competent. I asked Uncle William what that word meant after Mama went to jail. He said, 'That fool of a judge was a-saying you wasn't smart enough to speak about your own mother.'"

"Oh, come on, now, Lydia," Mr. Hinkle said. "We all know that's not true." He winked at me.

I grinned at him. But then I got all tight inside again. "I want to do this for my mama, but I'm still afeared I won't be able to."

"Will you try, Lydia?" Miss Parker asked.

"Yes, ma'am. I'll try."

"That's all we can ask."

"But, Miss Parker—"

"Yes, Lydia."

"My mama and me, well, we ain't got—I mean, we don't have much money. I know lawyers cost lots of money excepten when the judge gives you one. I heard Uncle William say he wished he could afford to get a good one for Mama. I got me seventy-two cents saved up in a jar in my dresser drawer to call Mama. You can have that. And Uncle William and Aunt Ethel Mae was—I mean, were—

planning on buying me a new coat tomorrow. Maybe I could ask them to give me that money to give to you."

Miss Parker patted my hand. "Don't worry about that, Lydia. Sometimes lawyers take cases they believe are important pro bono—that means free of charge. Assuming your mother agrees, we're going to do an appeal, which means we are going to tell the judge why the first trial was unfair to your mother. I hope the judge agrees so she can get another trial. If this thing turns out the way I think it will, someday soon your mother's coming home."

Then Miss Parker hit her fist on Mr. Hinkle's desk. "On top of that, we're going to sue that hospital for telling your mother to sign the papers without reading them and having her questions answered. I am going to do everything in my power to make sure that hospital doesn't treat anyone the way it treated your mother. If everything turns out the way I hope it will, your mother is going to have more money than she's ever had."

I didn't care so much about the money, but I sure liked hearing them words "coming home."

22

*It's about telling Uncle William
and Aunt Ethel Mae.*

TUESDAY, DECEMBER 22, 1953

A lot of things sure have changed since I talked to Mr.
Hinkle and Miss Parker. On the way home from school
yesterday, I stopped to pat that big brown dog down the
street. Him and me is friends now. I call him Ears on account of him having one big ear that sticks straight up on
the right side, and another big ear that folds over like it's
half asleep on the other side. I don't know what name his
master calls him, but he seems to like Ears just fine.

I told Ears I couldn't figure out iffen I should tell my
uncle and aunt that I went and disgraced them again by
talking to Mr. Hinkle and Miss Parker. Ears turned his
head sideways, a-listening real close to me. His eyes stared
into mine. "You're right, Ears. I need to recollect what

167

Mama taught me. 'Do the right thing, and everthing else will fall into place.' It's kind of confusing, though. You know what I mean? Me and Mama done the right thing about BJ, and that sure ain't fell into place." I sighed a big sigh. Ears licked my face. He knowed just exactly what I meant.

Miss Parker said it was up to me to decide. I could tell Uncle William and Aunt Ethel Mae, or she would tell them after she talked to Mama. When I was done talking it out with Ears, I knowed what I needed to do.

When I got home, I told Aunt Ethel Mae I would make supper and do the dishes all by myself and she could rest, even though I sure felt terrible wore out from spilling all them secrets to Mr. Hinkle and Miss Parker. But I knowed I best get Aunt Ethel Mae in a good mood. "Thank you kindly, Lydia," she said. "I have been feeling a smidgen under the weather today."

After supper, I announced that I had something real important to tell them. My hands was all shaky. I sat on the couch and pushed my hands under my legs to keep them quieted down. And then I told them all about Mr. Hinkle and Miss Parker and me talking about Mama after school. Aunt Ethel Mae started up crying, like I knowed she would. Uncle William just stared at me. I couldn't tell what he was a-thinking.

When I finally got done a-spitting it all out, Aunt Ethel Mae said, "Oh, Lydia, how could you—"

"Hush up, woman," Uncle William said. "Lydia, this

lawyer-woman—she really thinks she can help your mother?"

"Yes, sir," I said.

"Then we'll listen to what she has to say," Uncle William said as he got up from his chair and headed for the bedroom. Aunt Ethel Mae started to follow him.

"Wait, there's one more thing," I said.

Uncle William turned around. "What is it now?" he asked.

"Because of what I done and all, iffen you don't want to get me a new coat, it don't make me no never mind," I said.

"Don't you need a coat?" Uncle William asked.

"Yes, sir, I do."

"Well, it's done settled, then." He yawned and stretched. "I'm heading to bed."

I couldn't hold back no more. I runned and gived each of them a hug. "Thank you so very much," I said. When I hugged Uncle William, I felt like I hugged a statue. He patted me real quick on the back and then pulled away.

When I hugged Aunt Ethel Mae, she grinned. "Be careful, child," she said. "You're going to squeeze a body to death!" But she squeezed me back.

Aunt Ethel Mae and me went by bus to Charleston this afternoon. We stopped in Kresge's, and I had a barbecue with lots of coleslaw on it. I also got my steamy cup of hot chocolate with whipped cream and a cherry. Aunt Ethel

Mae ordered the blue plate special—a bowl of pinto beans with onions, fried taters, and a order of coleslaw. She got corn bread and coffee for free.

I tried to find a coat at the Diamond, but they cost way too much money. I had me some fun looking around in that fancy store, though. We tried J. C. Penney's, but O. J. Morrison's had the coat I liked best that didn't cost too much. It's blue—the color of BJ's and Mama's eyes, just what I wanted.

When I tried the coat on, Aunt Ethel Mae got tears in her eyes. "Oh, honey, you look so pretty and growed up in that coat. I didn't realize how much you be developing. I think we best pick you up a couple of brassieres while we's here. A young woman has to keep them little titties pushed up or they's going to be a-dragging on the floor afore she's marrying age." I know I turned mater red. It sure was embarrassing having to try them things on with Aunt Ethel Mae and the saleslady watching to make sure they fit right. But like Aunt Ethel Mae said, "We's all women."

Aunt Ethel Mae picked up a few things, too. Then we went to the big library to wait for Uncle William to meet us after work. I love that library. They's books on everthing you could ever think of. They even had a whole bunch of books about Anne of Green Gables. Aunt Ethel Mae let me get a library card and check out three books. She checked out a couple herself on gardening. I asked her how we would return them. "Well, I guess that means your uncle's just going to have to let me and you come to

170

Charleston again next month," she said. Then Aunt Ethel Mae winked at me. She really and truly did.

Uncle William parked close to the library. By the time we met him, the sky was dark and snow was a-falling. Them stores all stayed open late for Christmas, so we walked around downtown, looking at the lights and the windows all decorated up. We even seen the Salvation Army band. I still didn't have enough money to call Mama, but I figured I'd get to talk to her real soon anyways. I dropped a quarter in the bucket.

23

It's about Ears and Germy.

Ever day after school, I give Ears some of my lunch sandwich I save for him. He's a good dog, that one. When he sees me, his bushy tail starts going round and round like the electric fan Mr. Hinkle has at school. His tongue hangs out one side of his mouth, and his eyes light up like kerosene lamps. Of course, I ain't figured out for sure whether he's gladdest to see me or my lunch pail. He is kind of skinny.

He come a-bounding up to me today when he seen me walk down the road. "Sit!" I ordered him when he got close to me. And sit he did, just like a little soldier. I learned him to do that so's he wouldn't jump up on my new coat and get it all dirty. He learned to sit mighty fast.

Ears is a real smart dog. I showed him how to lie down, roll over, and shake hands. He does all them things for me, just 'cause I ask him. And on account of giving him pieces of my sandwich.

He was special excited to see me today. He wiggled from head to toe and whimpered and barked like he was a-trying his best to talk to me. He probably asked me, "Where in blazes have you been at, Lydia?" During Christmas break, I had to stay inside a lot with Aunt Ethel Mae. Today was my first day back to school in 1954.

When I went to the company store over the break for Aunt Ethel Mae, I bought Ears some Christmas presents with the money I had saved up. In my left pocket I had me a rubber ball. In my right pocket I had me a new comb. In my lunch pail, I had me a small poke filled with dog biscuits.

I could hear Ears' stomach growl. His eyes was like the eyes on one of them store-bought baby dolls, staring wide and straight at my lunch pail, never blinking at all. I opened it, and Ears started up licking his chops. I throwed him my leftover sandwich, and he gulped it down in one bite. "Good catch," I told him, and gived him a pat on the head.

He wagged his tail.

"Look what else I brung you. A surprise!" I pulled out a dog biscuit.

His tail wagged even faster. And some drool dropped on my shoe. I had him sit up for his treat.

Then I pulled out the rubber ball. His eyes glued onto

it like it was his ticket to Heaven! I wiggled it back and forth and up and down. Ain't no way his eyes would let it out of his sight. Finally, I pulled the ball behind me and throwed it as hard as I could. "Go get it, boy!" I said.

He shot off and brung the ball back all slobbery. Dogs is great, but they sure be messy sometimes. I throwed it a few more times. Then I used the hankie to wipe the ball and put it back in my pocket.

Ears turned his head to one side and looked at me all sad-like.

"That's it for today," I told him as I gived his head a quick pat. Then I pulled out the comb. I'm glad he's a big dog so I can comb him standing up and not mess up my clothes. He shivered like it felt good.

I combed and combed his coat and talked and talked. Ears listened real good to what I had to say. I told him about everthing that happened over Christmas. How Aunt Ethel Mae and Uncle William and me had fun shopping for my coat. And how on Christmas, Uncle William went straight out and put my dice on his car mirror. He said he liked them much better than store-bought ones. Aunt Ethel Mae loved her hankies with flowers so much that she got all tearful and used one of them to dab her eyes.

The best thing, I told Ears, was that Uncle William and Miss Parker spent a lot of time talking. She said it was important that him and me didn't talk to Mama afore the trial—something about influencing our testimony, whatever that means. Mama told her to tell me that she loved me. Mama said what I done about getting her a appeal was the best Christmas present I ever could of got her. Ears gived me a big doggy smile and spun his electric fan tail. He was right happy about them good things that had happened, too!

He turned his head sideways and shut his mouth when I told him about what I done today. I think Ears was real surprised. I thought a lot about what Mama told BJ to do when people is mean—that it's best to laugh at yourself. So I took the Sears and Roebuck catalog to school, the one that comed to Uncle William in the mail.

Mr. Hinkle weren't in class yet, so I walked over to Cora Lee's desk with the catalog open. Real loud so them other kids could hear, I said, "Cora Lee, you want me to have a new dress, so I picked out this one that you can buy me. See? It's right pretty. I picked out some shoes you can buy me, too."

Them kids all started up laughing. Cora Lee's mouth hung open so wide you could put a fist in it. "I'm just joshing you, Cora Lee," I said. "It was right nice that you wanted to help me. Thanks." Them kids clapped their hands, and Cora Lee grinned. I had me a big smile plastered on my face when I walked back to my seat. I told Ears that Maggie leaned over and asked me iffen she could sit with me at lunch. I told her, "Sure." Ears wagged his tail and barked when I finished the story. I think that's as close to doggy laughing as he could get.

After Ears was all combed out, I knowed I had to leave him behind again. I let out a long sigh. I cleaned the hair out of the comb the best I could and wrapped it in my hankie. Then I put it in my pocket. "It's time for me to go, Ears."

His eyes got all sad and droopy when he looked at me.

I gave him one more pat on the head and turned to walk away. I took a few steps toward Uncle William's house. I knowed Ears was a-following me. He always did.

"You go on home, now. You hear?" I put my hands on my hips and gave him a teacher look. I hated to do that.

Both of Ears' ears went down and back. He hung his head, put his tail between his legs, and headed on home. Poor Ears. I knowed what he didn't—that I would see him again tomorrow.

Anne of Green Gables had herself a person friend for her kindred spirit. I got me a kindred dog friend instead.

I wish BJ could've had hisself a dog. He wanted one real bad. Mama and Gran used to talk about how they wished they could get him a dog. It just weren't possible with us having to go up to Ohio all the time. We even had to give my cat, Hessie, away to some neighbors after we found out BJ was so sick. But BJ was bound and determined that he would have hisself a pet.

When we went up to Ohio, I looked down at BJ's pillowcase with his stuff in it. It laid on the floor between us in the backseat.

All at once, I seen something moving around in it.

BJ stuck his hand over my mouth afore I could scream.

Mama and Gran was a-talking up a blue streak up front. They didn't even turn around.

176

"What is it?" I mouthed them words to BJ but didn't make no sound.

He put one finger to his lips to tell me to *shhhh*. Then he reached his hand down into the pillowcase and pulled out the head of a black snake.

I put my own hand over my mouth to keep from screaming. I ain't afeared of black snakes. I know they's good snakes. But I sure weren't thinking about seeing one in a pillowcase on the way to Ohio!

BJ made his *shhhh* signal again. Then he shoved the snake back in his pillowcase and tied the top of it back into a knot. I just stared at him with my mouth a-hanging open.

We stopped at a service station that had a couple of picnic tables to eat the lunch Mama had packed for us. I grabbed BJ's arm and told Mama we was going to go get the key for the restroom.

"BJ, what in the name of all that is good and righteous do you think you are doing taking a black snake to Ohio?" I said when we got out of earshot.

"I got me a pet, Lyddie. I found him in the backyard yesterday. I named him Germy."

"Germy?"

"Yep. Anytime Jake and I start up exploring and playing in the hospital, Nurse Chapel grabs us by the ears and makes us go back to bed. 'You're going to get germy,' she says. So I decided she was right. Now I got Germy." He grinned real big.

I couldn't help but giggle. "BJ, how in the world do you think you're going to keep a snake in the hospital? What are you going to feed Germy?"

"I got it all figured out. Two of them books they have in that library at the hospital explain about reptiles. I read both of them three times. Germy's going to live under the covers with me to keep him warm and feeling safe. The sheets will keep him tucked in. Snakes is supposed to eat rodents. They probably got mice in that hospital, but I can't let Germy run around to find them. I'm going to give him mystery meat."

"Mystery meat?"

"Yep. That's what all us kids call the meat they serve us in the hospital. The way I figure it is this. 'Snakes find their prey by body heat and movement.' That's what the books said. I'm going to roll up hot balls of mystery meat and toss them around my bed. That way, Germy will think the mystery meat is a rodent and have hisself some supper. I always have water in a pitcher beside my bed that I can share with him. When the nurse is out of the room, I'll let him crawl around the floor and lay in the windowsill to get some sunshine. The other kids will help me."

I had to admit, he did seem to have it all figured out.

"You won't tell nobody, will you, Lyddie?" He gave me puppy-dog eyes.

I sighed. "Okay, I won't tell. But you best make sure Germy stays safe."

"I will. I be the kind of boy that always takes good care of his pets."

178

I didn't say nothing to Mama or Gran. I figured Germy would keep BJ real good company in the hospital.

We was a-sitting out on the porch three days later when Doc Smythson stopped by. He held his side and laughed all the way from his jeep to our cabin. Tears comed out of his eyes. We was all wide-eyed watching him.

"Do you know what that boy of yours did?" Doc Smythson said when he got to the porch.

"What now?" Gran asked. She rolled her eyes and shook her head.

Uh-oh. I figured I knowed what was a-coming.

"I got a call at the office from the hospital. They said they thought you should know what happened. Nurse Chapel stopped by BJ's ward early this morning to check on the kids. All of them were still asleep. When she got to BJ's bed, she thought for sure she saw something moving under the covers down at the foot of the bed, below BJ's feet. She pulled off the covers, and apparently screamed bloody murder, 'Snake! Snake! Snake!'

"All the staff in the hallway come running into the ward. The kids all woke up screaming because her screaming scared them. BJ started shouting, 'Don't hurt Germy! Don't hurt Germy!' Nurse Chapel ran out of the room long before the janitor came in to get the snake. BJ held Germy under his pajama top, still yelling at everyone not to hurt the snake. He started crying and coughing. An administrator came in and said they would let BJ take the snake off the property and turn it loose, to get him settled down."

We all laughed so hard we was a-crying by that time. I

thought BJ should be right proud that he kept Germy for three days afore Nurse Chapel found him.

BJ told me all about it when he comed home from the hospital. He said Nurse Chapel could of won herself a trophy at a clogging competition when she saw Germy, the way she danced around, barely letting her feet touch the floor.

BJ got to ride in a little cart with the janitor to turn Germy loose. Him and the janitor got to be good friends, talking about the snake the janitor had when he was a boy. He also knowed all about motors and told BJ how the cart worked. They found a great home for Germy with lots of tall grass, a little pond, and good-tasting Ohio mice for dinner. BJ said it was a good thing, because Germy was probably getting mighty hungry. Germy didn't like that mystery meat any better than them kids did.

The best thing, BJ told me, was that Nurse Chapel got herself transferred to another hospital that just had adults for patients. He never had to see her again.

After saying good-bye to Ears, I kept thinking about BJ and his snake as I walked to Uncle William's house. All at once I heard laughing and figured out that the noise comed from me. It surprised me. I ain't heard myself laugh like that for a long time.

But I sure caught it good from Aunt Ethel Mae when I walked in the door.

"Lydia, you should have been here over half an hour ago. Have you been out playing with that smelly dog again and me here with a sick headache worrying about you? You might get rabies from that mutt. And who knows where his mouth has been. Dogs wipe theirselves with their tongues, you know. . . ."

On and on she went. Ain't no one going to make you change your mind about a kindred spirit, though. I walked over to her whilst she still jabbered away about poor old Ears and kissed her on the cheek. She hushed up and got all wide-eyed and slack-jawed. Then she reached her hand up and touched where I had kissed her.

I smiled at her and walked to my room. I could feel her eyes a-following me all the way.

24

It's about not knowing who I be no more.

I never understood what folks meant when I heard them say, "No good deed goes unpunished." But I think I understand now. Today I tried to do a good deed and my whole life won't never be the same again.

Aunt Ethel Mae always keeps everthing neat and clean where people can see—and that's most of this little house. But she also has herself what she likes to call junk drawers. They's full of most everthing you can think of. Them drawers sure be hard to open. You have to poke your fingers inside and scoot stuff around to pull them out. And then when you try to close them, stuff spills out on the floor and you have to scoot everthing around again and shove hard to finally get them junk drawers shut.

When I got home from school today, Aunt Ethel Mae had one of them bad headaches. She was in bed with a cold washcloth on her head. "Lydia," she called to me real feeble-like from her bedroom, "I been sick all day and couldn't pull myself out of bed to do the ironing. Do you think you could be a good girl and help me out with it?"

I had me a bunch of homework and was glad she couldn't see me roll my eyes. I just said sure, put my books on my bed, and commenced to sorting the laundry basket after I put a stew on the stove for supper. I ironed the shirts, trousers, dresses, and blouses first to get them hard clothes out of the way. Then I ironed the skirts and hung all the clothes in the bedrooms. I saved the cotton napkins and Sunday tablecloth for last. When they was pressed and folded, I went to put them away in the little buffet that's under the window in the living room.

I needed to put the napkins and tablecloth in the bottom drawer, but the top drawer stuck out some with stuff pouring out of it like paper molasses. Try as I might, I couldn't get the stuff shoved back in to close the drawer. So I decided to pull it out and set it on the floor. I figured I could get rid of any trash and try to sort the rest of it so I wouldn't have to keep fighting it any time I needed to put things away. I thought I might as well take out the bottom drawer and sort it, too.

When I pulled out the bottom drawer, I saw a envelope taped to the back of the buffet. The envelope and the tape was yellow, like they been hanging there with no one seeing them for years. I started to reach for the envelope, but then I pulled my hand back. I thought of Gran saying, "Curiosity killed the cat." But I knowed that Hessie lived after being curious about most everthing. Besides, I figured no one would ever know. I was as drawed to that envelope as Eve was to the apple.

I reached my hand out again. I wish I had recollected the story we heard tell of in Mr. Hinkle's class when we studied mythology. We read about a lady named Pandora. She opened a box that changed everthing in the world, and not in a good way. As soon as I gently rubbed my finger behind that tape to loosen it, I had commenced to open Pandora's box.

The envelope wasn't sealed. The flap was tucked instead, so I figured it was safe to look at what was inside. Then I could stick the envelope to the buffet again when I finished. I pulled out the paper and set the envelope on the floor aside me.

The paper was folded in thirds. Nothing was wrote on the back. When I unfolded it, a picture of a woman fell out. I glanced at it and laid it aside. Then I read what was wrote on the paper, and my heart stopped. The whole world stopped. It was a birth certificate from the State of West Virginia. And there was my name. Well, almost my name. And my birth date. But not my mother's and father's names.

The name on the birth certificate said *Lydia Jane Garton*—not *Lydia Jane Hawkins*. The birth date: *March 15, 1942*. Father's name: *William Stanley Garton*—my uncle's name and Gran's last name. Mother's name: *Helen*

Jane Garton. I didn't know who that woman could be. It sure ain't Aunt Ethel Mae. And it sure ain't my mama.

I picked up the picture again. It didn't have no name or date on it. The woman smiled at me from the picture— a nice smile. She was pretty in a gentle way. I couldn't tell the color of her hair or eyes on account of the picture being black-and-white, but they looked dark. Her hair hung down in long curls around her shoulders. And I saw she had freckles—soft little spots that seemed to make her beauty real special, not like the beauty other folks have.

No one else in the family has freckles but me. Tears runned down my face. Was my mama not my mama? What could this mean?

I heard a car parking in front of the house and knowed it was my uncle.

I stuffed the birth certificate and picture back in the envelope. I tried to stick the envelope to the back of the buffet, but the tape wouldn't stick no more. I smoothed out the stuff in the drawers the best I could and shoved them in the buffet. Then I slid the envelope behind the elastic in my skirt and hid it under my blouse, just as I heard my uncle opening the back door. I stepped into the kitchen, picked up the spoon, and stirred the stew as he stepped into the kitchen.

"William, is that you, sweetheart?" Aunt Ethel Mae called even more feeble than she did to me. "Come give me a kiss after you clean up, dear." Uncle William rolled his eyes just like I had. He took off his work boots and dropped them on the mat at the door. He took off his dirty socks and put them in his pants pocket. Then he dropped his lunch bucket and thermos on the kitchen table, trudged to the bathroom to take a quick shower to get rid of the coal dust, trudged into the bedroom to give Aunt Ethel Mae her kiss, and listened to her complain about her headache—or at least pretended to listen.

I breathed a sigh of relief and started spooning the stew into three bowls. The warm salty smell of stew makes me hungry most times, but not tonight. My stomach was too balled up. I poured milk and coffee, cut some bread, got out the butter and jam, and set the table for Uncle William and me. I dished up some peaches for dessert. Then I made up a tray for Aunt Ethel Mae and took it to her.

When I sat down at the table to eat supper with Uncle William, the envelope rubbed against me, making me itch. I worried that Uncle William might notice it bulging under my blouse and maybe worried just a little that he *wouldn't* see it. But he brought the *Daily Mail* to the table with him. Uncle William read that newspaper the whole time he was eating and didn't even look at me once. When he finished eating, he grunted, "Good stew, Lydia," got up from the table, turned on the radio in the living room, sprawled hisself out on the couch, let out a big belch, fell asleep, and commenced to snoring.

I went to pick up the tray from Aunt Ethel Mae. "Come here and sit on the bed," she whimpered like a pup. "Tell me about your day, Lydia." I sat down with the envelope making my blouse stick out like it wanted to be noticed. But Aunt Ethel Mae didn't see nary a thing.

I knowed how this would go. It's like Aunt Ethel Mae is always trying to find her way in one of them houses of mirrors they have at fairs. No matter where she looks, she only sees herself. "School was fine," I said, not looking her in the eye.

"I recollect when I was your age . . . ," she said, looking out the little window. And then on and on and on she talked.

When she finally stopped to take a breath, I said, "Well, I guess I best finish the dishes and get to my homework." I figured she had got her talking out of her system. She let me leave.

Uncle William sat on the couch crocheting a red, white, and blue afghan. I ain't sure what he done with them afghans now that Mama is in prison. Maybe he took them to work and gived them away. I feel right certain that he wouldn't tell them miners he be the one that crocheted them. I also reckon that any of them miners that made fun of Uncle William would hurt pretty bad for a few days. Maybe Aunt Ethel Mae gived them to her church. Iffen she did, I bet she bragged that she made them. I sure wasn't going to ask him about it.

I stood by the couch and watched him wiggle them big needles back and forth for a couple of minutes, but he never looked up. Part of me wanted to talk to him about what I found. But the biggest part was too afeared.

As I cleaned up the kitchen, I wished I could wash away that birth certificate just as easy as I washed the dirt offen them dishes.

I kept a-trying to sort it all out while my hands was busy with the dishes. Iffen that birth certificate is real, this is the way I worked it out. Mama and Daddy is my aunt and uncle. BJ is my cousin and not my brother. Gran and Gramps was still my grandparents when they was alive. Uncle William is my real daddy and Aunt Ethel Mae is my stepmother. That last one was a real scary thought. And what happened to my real mama?

I felt as empty as the jam jar I washed out. All that I knowed about myself was gone. My tears added to the dishwater. I understood then about how Aunt Ethel Mae felt with her sick headaches. I opened the cabinet and got out the bottle of aspirins. I wondered what would happen iffen I took all of them. But I took out one little pill and swallowed it with a glass of water.

Gran always told me I whizzed out of Mama like a pellet from a shotgun—real easy. Mama told me when I came to be, I was her only star in a dark, dark sky. I recollect them telling me that as clear as iffen it happened today. Why did they lie to me? I felt this anger come up inside me like hot, red lava from one of them volcanoes that Mr. Hinkle showed us a filmstrip about. I wanted to let it spew out over everone.

I had to know. Somebody had to tell me the truth. As afeared as the thought made me, I knowed that one person had to be Uncle William. When I fixed Uncle William's lunch for tomorrow, I filled his thermos with coffee and the bottom container of his heavy metal lunch bucket with water. I wrapped two tuna fish salad sandwiches in wax paper and tucked them and a apple in the middle container. I wrapped a piece of blackberry pie for the top container. I also folded the envelope with the birth certificate in half, making sure I didn't fold the picture. I wrapped it in wax paper and put it underneath the pie. Aunt Ethel Mae once told me coal miners always eat dessert first in case something bad happens to them. I wanted to make sure Uncle William seen that there envelope afore he had one bite to eat.

25

It's about what Uncle William told me.

FRIDAY, FEBRUARY 5, 1954

After school today, Mr. Hinkle asked me iffen I was okay. He said it wasn't like me not to do my homework and that I seemed very quiet. I told him I was sorry and that I hadn't felt well.

"Are you concerned about the trial, Lydia?" he asked as he patted my shoulder.

"A little," I said. How could I begin to tell him everthing I was worried about?

"Well, that's understandable. I need you to try to stay caught up with your work, though. We don't want you getting behind."

"I'll get caught up tonight," I promised.

I sure was glad to see Ears trotting up to me when I

walked home from school. I sat down on the curb aside him and buried my head in his neck. I wrapped my arms real tight around him. His body tensed up like he was asking me, "What's wrong?" He licked my face. I couldn't talk, not even to him.

Me and him sat together until he had licked all the tears offen my face. I patted him for a bit. Then I said, "You and me be alike, Ears. You seem to think you belong to me, but you really belong to the people in that house over there. I don't know who I belong to, neither." Ears whimpered a little like he knowed what I meant.

I was just about to stand up and finish walking to the house when I saw my uncle's car coming around the corner. My heart started beating so fast I thought I might faint. I wanted to run, but I was like a rabbit trapped by a bobcat—too afeared to move. Uncle William pulled the car over and opened the door on my side.

"Get in," he ordered. Ears barked at him.

My voice shook, but I said, "Go home, Ears," and pointed to his house. Ears looked like he didn't want to leave me alone. But he did what I told him.

I climbed in the car with my uncle. He didn't say nothing. I didn't, neither. He drove to his house, parked the car, and told me, "Stay put."

I did. I twirled a strand of my hair and was surprised to see I had pulled a few hairs out of my head. I didn't even feel it.

Uncle William got back in the car and handed me the shopping list. "I told your aunt that I took off a couple of hours early to get some hunting supplies at Sears and Roe-buck for this weekend. I picked you up on the way home and figured I could drop you at Evans to do the grocery shopping. She said she wanted to go shopping, but I told her she needed to stay home on account of being so sick. I said I would bring her something."

I knowed Aunt Ethel Mae wouldn't be happy about that, but I didn't say nothing. She loves to shop at Sears and Roebuck. I wondered iffen Uncle William got in trouble for taking off early. I wanted to ask him what he told his boss, but I was afeared to.

Was we really going shopping? I pulled out a few more strands of hair thinking about it. We drove offen the hill and turned left toward Charleston. Then Uncle William pulled over at a little park at Hometown.

It ain't much of a park, just a couple of picnic tables and signs. One tells how George Washington acquired all the land up in these parts. His nephew lived close to the park in Red House. The other one tells how the highway was the path of a Colonial army that defeated Cornstalk at Point Pleasant. I knowed all that because we took a field trip to the park when I was in fourth grade. We even had a picnic after we read and talked about the signs. I figured me and Uncle William weren't going to have no picnic.

"Get out," Uncle William ordered me.

I got out. At least I knowed he wouldn't hit me. Too many cars kept passing by. He sat hisself down at one of the picnic tables. I sat down across from him. I shivered and my teeth chattered. I don't know whether it was because it was so cold or on account of being so afeared of him. I pushed my hands deeper in the pockets of the coat he bought me. Most times the smell of cold air makes me feel clean inside. Today it just made me feel numb.

Uncle William looked hot. His face was all red. "How did you find it?" His steel-blue eyes drilled holes in me.

I told him without looking at his face. I stared at a knothole in the picnic table as I forced them words out of my mouth.

"You had no right to open that envelope!" he yelled, and slammed his fist on the table.

I jumped like he had slammed that fist down on me. Tears ran fast down my cheeks. I covered my face with my hands. My gloves caught the tears, but now my hands was wet. "I'm sorry, I'm sorry," I moaned.

He stood up and walked away from me. I watched him through my fingers. He put his arm on a oak tree that was dead of leaves for winter and leaned his head on his arm. He stayed that way for a while. Then he comed back to the table and sat down.

He sighed. "What do you want to know, Lydia?"

I still didn't look at him, but the tears stopped coming. "Is my mama my real mama?"

He didn't say nothing for a while. Then he said, "Yes, Lydia. Your mama is your real mama. But she's not your birth mother."

"The lady in the picture is my birth mother?"

"That's right."

"Are you my daddy?"

193

"No, I'm your uncle William by law."

"What do you mean?"

"I gived you up to your parents for adoption soon after you was borned."

I tried to imagine what my life would have been like iffen I had growed up with Uncle William. I couldn't even get a tiny picture of it in my head. "You didn't want me?" I asked.

Uncle William fidgeted a little and then cleared his throat like he had to make room for the words to come out of his mouth. He didn't look at me when he talked. "Helen—your birth mother—and I wanted you more than anything." He thought for a bit. Then he said, "I dropped out of high school to take a job in a machine shop in Charleston. Times was tough, and I wanted to get out on my own and make my own way. I had me a little one-room apartment. I ate at Jack's Place most days. That's where I met Helen. She worked there as a waitress."

"You thought she was pretty?"

"Beautiful. She always had a smile for me. I could talk to her."

That was saying something. I knowed how hard it was for Uncle William to talk to anybody about anything. "So you married her."

"Yeah. We eloped. Most folks couldn't afford a fancy wedding back then. We didn't have much money, but we saved up what we could for a house. We was real happy when we found out Helen was going to have a baby. I didn't know nothing about raising young'uns, but I knowed Helen would help me learn. She loved kids—always talked to them and liked to give them special treats when they comed in the restaurant."

"What happened to her? Where is she?"

Another real long sigh blowed out of him and his face tightened up. "She died, Lydia. They had a special waiting area at the hospital for what they called expectant fathers. After a time, the doctor called my name and took me to another room. He said you come out fine but your mother didn't make it." One tear crept out of his eye. It didn't slide down his face very far until he pushed it aside with his sleeve and cleared his throat again.

My throat got tight. "I killed my mother?"

He looked me straight in the eyes. "It ain't right for you to think of it like that, Lydia. Helen never would have wanted you to see it that way."

"But iffen I hadn't been borned, she would still be here. Is that why you gived me away? You hated me for killing her?" I cried again. I was shivering hard.

"No, Lydia. It ain't like that." He looked at me for a minute. "Come on. Let's go back to the car, and I'll put the heater on. We'll finish our talk there."

So we walked back to the car. It took a few minutes for the heater to warm up. We didn't say nothing for a while.

"You was borned three months after the Japanese attacked Pearl Harbor," Uncle William started up again. "You know about World War Two, right?"

I nodded without looking at him.

"I wanted to do my part to make the world safe for

195

you and Helen. I enlisted in the Army Air Corps a month after Pearl Harbor. I would have been drafted anyhow, so I wanted to choose the branch where I would serve. I knowed that Helen could take care of you on the money I made in the service. I thought I could take the two of you with me wherever I had training in the States afore going overseas. Helen thought it would be a adventure to live in another state. You was borned in March. I was scheduled to leave in May."

"You couldn't get out of it to take care of me?"

"No, Lydia. I couldn't. War don't work like that. A lot of soldiers died in that war. I didn't know iffen I would come back. I thought about leaving you with my folks, but they was getting up in years. I tried to figure out what was best for you. I knowed that Sarah would be the best mother a young'un could ever have. Her and me both got married just a few months apart. John was 4-F and couldn't be drafted. Iffen I gived you to them, you would have a mother and father to love you and care for you. I signed the adoption papers for them to take you."

"Did you try to get me back when you comed home?"

"I had signed them papers, Lydia. You seemed real happy with Sarah. It felt best to leave you with her. It took me a while to figure out what to do with myself when I got back."

"You become a coal miner," I said, still trying to sort it all out.

He nodded. "I thought about getting my GED and going to college on the GI Bill—maybe be a chemist.

196

They's good jobs for chemists in Charleston. But I took a job in the coal mine so I could be close to Mom after Dad died, in case she needed me. I sent her part of my check each month. And then Sarah and John moved in with her."

"I loved being with Mama, but Daddy was real scary sometimes," I said. I looked out the car window, but I didn't see nothing but my thoughts.

"What?" I could feel Uncle William stare at me hard.

I looked at him, surprised. "You know. When he got liquored up."

His hands was on the steering wheel. He balled them into fists. "Did he ever hit you, Lydia?"

"No, I hid when he got like that. But he hit Mama and Gran sometimes."

Uncle William stared out the windshield like he was a-trying his best to see Daddy. His hands tightened up until they looked like rocks. "Iffen I had knowed that, I would of killed that son of a . . ." He looked at me. "I would of put a stop to it. He died in that accident about a year after I got out of the service. It would have been sooner iffen I had knowed."

I figured out then why Mama and Gran didn't tell him about Daddy. Uncle William would have killed him and ended up in jail or maybe even worse. I wondered again about the plan they had to get away from Daddy. I figured I best change the subject.

"I recollect when you and Aunt Ethel Mae got married," I said. "I was your flower girl."

His hands opened up again. "Yeah. You done real good tossing them rose petals up the church aisle. Everbody thought you was real cute."

I smiled, but just a little. "Do you love Aunt Ethel Mae as much as you loved Helen?"

He frowned and gived it some thought. "You can love people for different things and in different ways, Lydia. Ethel Mae was a lot of fun when I met her, and I sure did need some fun in my life. I could talk to Helen. But when I met Ethel Mae, I didn't want to do much talking. I knowed Ethel Mae would do all the talking that needed to be done."

I had a hard time picturing Aunt Ethel Mae being much fun. But then I thought about the night we had ice cream when it was cold outside. I sure don't think that was Uncle William's idea. "Does Aunt Ethel Mae know about Helen?"

"Yeah, but she doesn't know about you being Helen's daughter. I thought a lot about this. Iffen Sarah comes home, I know beyond a shadow of a doubt that you belong with her." He looked at me like he was trying to see inside my head. "I will always be there for you, any way I can, Lydia. Iffen your mama don't come home, you will always have a home with me. Do you understand what I'm a-telling you?"

I nodded. I was still all confused with everthing, but I understood them words he said.

Some of the wrinkles eased out of his face. "I hate to put this on you, Lydia, but you must keep this a secret from your aunt Ethel Mae. Will you promise not to tell her or anyone else?"

I felt queasy thinking about having to keep all this bottled up inside. "I promise," I said. I was glad Ears wasn't a person. At least I could confide to him.

"Good. I put the birth certificate and picture of Helen in a safe deposit box at the bank afore picking you up. That's what I should ought of done in the first place."

"Why did Gran and Mama lie to me?" I asked. "I remember Gran telling me that she tickled Mama's nose with a feather and I whizzed out of her like a pellet from a shotgun. Mama said I was her only shining star in a dark, dark sky when I comed to be."

He thought for a minute. Then he pushed some more words out, looking at me out of the corner of his eyes. "From what you told me about John, Sarah told you the truth. You probably asked Gran about being borned when BJ comed and Sarah was in the hospital. Your gran tried to spare you from something you was too little to understand. Most of the births she midwifed probably was that easy. Life ain't simple, Lydia. Most people want to do what's best for the people they care about. Sometimes it's just real hard to figure out what that be."

I nodded. It was still real hard to think of Gran lying to me. She was a good Christian lady. I figured I was going to have to think about this for a spell to sort it all out. I had me two more questions for Uncle William. "Am I like Helen?" I asked him.

Uncle William looked at my face and smiled at me for

the first time I could recollect. "You are ever bit as pretty and kind as she was. I see her ever time I look at you. Mr. Hinkle tells me you like to write and you're real good at it. Helen dreamed of being a writer. She used to write poems and stories. I always thought someday I would see a book of hers at the big library in Charleston. Maybe I'll see yours instead."

I smiled, too. "Where is she buried, Uncle William?"

He looked out the windshield again. "I knowed I would leave Kanawha County and move back to Putnam County after the war. Helen didn't have no brothers and sisters, and her parents died in a car wreck a few years afore we got married. So I buried her on Paradise Hill at the little cemetery on Bowles Ridge Road. I thought she would like it there. Some of the other Garton family is there, and I didn't have no ties with the church cemetery where your grandparents and BJ be buried. I didn't go to no church until Ethel Mae commenced to dragging me on Sunday mornings."

I nodded. Iffen Aunt Ethel Mae wants something, it's a lot easier to do it than listen to her fuss. I knowed where that road to the cemetery is. It ain't too far from my school.

"We best get them errands done," Uncle William said. "Your aunt's going to be fit to be tied by the time we get home."

We stopped at Sears and Roebuck first. I hurried to pick out a new scarf for Aunt Ethel Mae while Uncle William got his hunting supplies. We shopped together for the groceries at Evans, and then we went to Jack's Place on West Washington Street to get some hot dogs and French fries to take home for supper. We didn't talk no more about the birth certificate. Each time we got in the car to drive to the next place, Uncle William turned on the radio. My thoughts was a lot louder than the music.

It was about seven-thirty when we got home. Uncle William was right. Aunt Ethel Mae was fit to be tied.

26

It's about saying hello and good-bye.

Thursday, February 11, 1954

When you lose yourself, living ain't much more than doing the same things over and over. Get up in the morning. Go to school. Do the chores. Shove down some food. Do homework. Go to bed. Try to sleep. Then get up the next day and do it all again. Today I figured I had to do something different.

It's been a week since I found that birth certificate. Me and Uncle William ain't hardly looked at each other. We sure ain't mentioned the birth certificate no more. We both been acting like it don't exist.

Mr. Hinkle asked me again yesterday iffen I wanted to talk about the trial. He said he's worried about me on account that I've been so quiet and my grades has dropped.

On Monday, when Maggie sat down to eat lunch with me, I told her my stomach hurt. "Did Aunt Flo from Red River come to visit?" she asked. "Did she bring Gramps?" Maggie giggled. "Aunt Flo ain't visited me yet at all. I wish she would hurry up. I ain't even got titties yet. I been stuffing the brassiere my sister outgrowed with toilet paper. But don't you go telling no one that. Mom sleeps late, so she don't see me in the morning. She works at the beauty shop all day, so I take it off afore she gets home. I can't wait till I fill it out for real and them boys start to pay me some notice."

I thought her bosoms looked lopsided sometimes. Now I knowed why. I told her no, I ain't going to tell no one, and yes, Aunt Flo paid me a visit. I couldn't tell her the real reason why my stomach was all cramped up. Uncle William said I couldn't tell anyone about that birth certificate. It pained me to lie to Maggie.

Yesterday, Maggie said I ain't no fun no more. She ate lunch with them other girls instead of me. It didn't make me no never mind. I read one of my books from the library about Anne of Green Gables and tried to gag down a few bites of my sandwich.

Anne of Green Gables got herself adopted. But she knowed her parents died. And she knowed she wanted Marilla and Matthew to adopt her. She begged them to adopt her. I didn't know nothing about what happened to me. I didn't have no choice.

I kept on thinking how hard I been working to get Mama out of jail. But she never told me she didn't birth me. She let me think I was as much hers as BJ. Did she keep me to help take care of the kids she would have someday? Like Anne took care of other people's kids? Maybe she didn't really even love me. She just felt like she had to take care of me on account of Uncle William being her brother.

All I wanted since BJ died was to have Mama back with me. But after finding that birth certificate, I didn't know iffen I ever wanted to see her again. I wished I could just go off someplace and live on my own. But I would have to make money, and I knowed no one would hire a girl my age.

The Bible says the truth shall set you free. But the truth made me feel trapped—so trapped that my breath squeezed tight in my chest.

Today afore lunch, I told Mr. Hinkle that I must of caught a stomach bug. I asked to go on home. "Are you sure you are all right to walk home, Lydia?" he asked. "I could drive you if you could wait a half hour for our lunch break."

"No, I ain't that bad sick," I told him. "It ain't that far to walk."

He didn't even pull on his ear to remind me to use Standard English. He just wrinkled up his face like he was worried, nodded, and told me I could go iffen I was sure I could make it. So I walked out of school and toward Uncle William's house. But I didn't go there. I went to find Ears.

Ears jumped and ran in circles when he saw me. I think he was right surprised to see me that early. I slapped my leg to tell him to follow me. His tongue hung out the side of his mouth, and he doggy-grinned when he runned toward me. I ain't never let him follow me afore. I didn't care what them people that owned Ears thought. I needed my kindred spirit to go with me. They didn't seem to pay him much mind anyways.

It was sunny and not too cold. The snow we had a few days ago was melted. I felt real thankful for such a pretty day in the middle of winter. Me and Ears walked away from my uncle's house to Paradise. We had to walk past the school again. That meant we had to hike through the woods across the street.

When I didn't worry no more about them teachers and kids seeing us, I sat down on a dry rock in the sun to share my lunch with Ears. I ate a few bites of my baloney sandwich and gived Ears most of it. He gobbled down the extra sandwich I packed for him, too. He licked my hand when he was done to show me he was real grateful.

I knowed when I left for school this morning that I wouldn't get milk for lunch today, so I packed a jar of grape Kool-Aid in my lunch poke. I drunk that while Ears got hisself a drink out of a nearby puddle that wasn't froze over. I don't know how dogs can drink muddy water, but he drunk like it was chocolate milk, slopping it all over his face. Then he trotted to a nearby bush and raised his leg to leave his mark. He lifted his leg so high I thought he might topple over. He wanted to make sure his mark was higher than all them other dogs' marks. *He's all boy,* I thought, and couldn't help but laugh a little.

When he finished his business, Ears walked over and sat next to me. I had packed a extra hankie in my poke for a napkin, and I used it to wipe offen his slobbery doggy face. He didn't pull away, but he squirmed a bit like he couldn't figure out why I wanted to do that to him. When I finished, Ears plopped his big old head in my lap and looked up at me as if to say, "What's going on, Lydia?"

But I didn't bring him with me to talk to him. I needed to talk to somebody else. I just wanted Ears close to me. I patted his head for a bit and then leaned over and placed my head on top of his. I stroked his back. He sighed and leaned his body as close to mine as he could. I knowed I would probably have to use a whole roll of tape to get the dog hairs offen my new coat, but I didn't care one little bit.

We sat that way for a little while, Ears and me. Then I got up and headed for Bowles Ridge Road. Ears runned ahead and sniffed for interesting smells, bounding back to me from time to time for a quick pat on the head.

When I comed to the fence gate, I stopped to look at the little cemetery. Trees surrounded the back of the little hill. I imagine how pretty and peaceful the cemetery must be in the other seasons. In spring the blooming trees match the colors of the fresh flowers folks place on the graves. In summer, the heavy green leaves shelter them that rest in the ground. In the fall, the red, gold, and orange leaves provide a blanket for the graves. But today, in winter, the empty branches of the trees reached up to the blue sky like little children asking for God to pick them up in His arms.

I told Ears to stay and wait for me. I was afeared he might decide to mark a headstone afore I could stop him. That didn't seem very respectful of them that had passed on. Ears whimpered a little and looked up at me with sad brown eyes, but he stretched out on the ground with his head on his front paws and waited.

When I got inside, I laid my lunch poke down near the gate. I didn't have no idea where Helen's grave might be. I commenced to looking at the right side and moved toward the back, reading each headstone. Lots of Casto, Craigo, and Parker headstones dotted the hill. I finally found the Garton headstones near the front on the left side. Then I found the headstone I was a-looking for.

HELEN JANE GARTON

MAY 26, 1922–MARCH 15, 1942

MY SPIRIT FREES, AND I AM ONE WITH GOD.

The cemetery had some headstones for babies that died on the same day they was borned. A few had little lambs resting on top of the headstones. One had a toy wagon chiseled in the stone. Two of the babies died the same year Helen died. I could of died on my birth date, too. I could of had a little grave beside Helen's.

I shivered to think about it. Instead of being on Earth, I could be in Heaven now with BJ and Gran and Daddy.

And with Helen. I wondered iffen I would have been forever a baby in Heaven. Would I have growed up like I be on Earth? Is BJ forever a boy in Heaven? Helen's headstone says her spirit freed. I wondered iffen her spirit has freckles.

I touched the words on Helen's headstone and traced the letters with my fingers. My birth mother. This lady that I only seen in a picture. The body that she once owned laid here. Her spirit. Who she was inside. Who she still is with God. That's who I needed to speak to. The Bible says we are surrounded by a great cloud of witnesses. I hoped her spirit floated above me in that cloud and that she could hear me.

"I can't call you Mother, even though you birthed me," I whispered to her. "Even though you gived your life so that I could be. I can only call you Helen. I hope you understand. I only know one mama."

And then the tears clouded my eyes. I recollected all the good times I had when Mama and me sat on the porch and talked, and when Gran and me took our walks in the woods. "I only know one mama, and I love her," I said again to Helen. "Mama and Gran was always there for me. They didn't tell me the truth, but they done the best they could by me. They loved me with everthing they had inside them. Even Uncle William tries his best to make sure I have a good life."

I begun to sob out all the anger that had built up in me. When the sobbing finished, I felt clean inside. And I knowed that feeling was forgiveness. A soft voice spoke deep inside me: "Lydia, things are as they are meant to be." Was that Helen's voice? Or God's? Or was I telling myself them words? I didn't know for sure. But I felt safe and loved like I was nestled in a bird's wings.

I wiped my face with the hankie I kept in my coat pocket and looked up at the sky. "Thank you for my life, Helen," I said, and blowed a kiss toward Heaven.

Then I walked to the cemetery gate and didn't look back. Ears jumped up on the fence when he seen me coming. I glanced at the sun and knowed we would have to hurry to get back afore school let out. I took off at a run, and Ears barked and danced around me, glad for a race. When we comed to his house, I hugged him and thanked him for going with me today. He wagged his tail and licked my hand. Then I had to tell him to go on home. His eyes drooped low and his tail fell between his legs, but he went on home.

I runned the rest of the way to Uncle William's house and stopped to catch my breath afore walking through the front door. Aunt Ethel Mae had country music blaring from the radio and sung while she fixed supper. I said a prayer of thanks in my heart that she was in a good mood.

"I'm home," I said.

"How was school?" she asked.

"Fine." I hurried into my bedroom afore she had a chance to talk to me about anything else.

I heard a car pull up in front of the house almost as soon as I got to the bedroom. I looked out my window and saw Mr. Hinkle parking his car. My heart jumped up in my throat. I was sure glad that music was loud. I figured Aunt Ethel Mae couldn't hear the car from the kitchen. I slipped out the front door and met Mr. Hinkle as he got out of his car.

"Lydia," he said, "I wanted to make sure you arrived home safely. Are you feeling better?"

"Yes, much better," I said. That part was true.

"Maybe I could talk to your aunt while I'm here."

"She has one of her headaches, and she's taking a nap." That part was a lie. I wondered iffen he could hear the radio blaring and Aunt Ethel Mae belting out the tune. I hoped his hearing weren't as good as mine.

His eyebrows shot up, and he looked me in the eyes. "Well," he said, "I'm glad you're feeling better. Do you think you'll be able to come to school tomorrow?"

I nodded.

"Good. I brought your homework." He took my books from his car and handed them to me. "I wrote the assignments on a piece of paper in your math book." He smiled at me. I didn't smile back. "Tell your aunt I hope she feels better soon." He climbed into his car and drove away.

When I slipped through the front door, Aunt Ethel Mae was dancing as well as singing while she banged pans around on the stove. I rolled my eyes and went to my bedroom.

I sat on my bed and thought how I had lied to Mr. Hinkle twice today. And how I lied to Maggie. And how I lied on account of not knowing what else to do. Was that why everbody had lied to me? They didn't know what else

210

to do? They didn't know how to tell the truth without making things worse? I said a quick prayer for God to forgive me for them lies I been telling.

I wanted to take a nap. I felt heavy and tired like I could finally sleep. But I figured I best try to do my homework. I opened my math book. At the top of the page with my assignments, Mr. Hinkle wrote, "I believe in you, Lydia."

27

It's about dinner, singing, and Jake's mama.

Tomorrow is Mama's new trial. Ever since I went to the cemetery, I knowed that I want Mama back home. That's still my dream. And I knowed I want to live with her again. I feel confused about myself sometimes, and it troubles me that all I thought about who I be is gone. I wish Mama and Gran would of told me the truth.

I sure have changed a lot since Mama was took away from me. I wonder iffen Mama has changed. Will her and me be able to talk and feel close to each other after all we been through?

Miss Parker done a real good job for Mama with the appeal. The judge agreed to the reasons why Mama deserved another trial. Somebody else's trial needed to be changed, so the judge told Miss Parker a month ago that he had an opening tomorrow.

Miss Parker says she's real hopeful about this new trial. But she also says I ought to be prepared that Mama might not win this trial either. I don't know how I can be prepared for that.

Me and Uncle William and Aunt Ethel Mae drove up to Ohio yesterday morning. Miss Parker and Mr. Hinkle met us there. Pastor John and Doc Smythson comed up this evening to have dinner with us.

Miss Parker reserved us a room at a real nice hotel. It's called a suite. I have my own bedroom. It's the fanciest place I ever slept in my life. Miss Parker even paid for it. She said when Mama wins her civil case against the hospital, we can pay her back iffen we want.

That hotel even had one of them newfangled television sets in the lobby. It sure is weird seeing little fuzzy gray people moving across that there box. Them people's voices come right out of the box, too, just like on the radio.

I don't think them television sets be for me. You have to stare at the picture. I like to move around and do stuff when I listen to the radio. Besides, I make much better pictures in my head than the pictures of them people on that little screen. And my head pictures be full of colors!

Yesterday afternoon after we got settled in at the hotel, I went shopping with Miss Parker for a new outfit to help give me confidence. We went to a big store call Lazarus. Aunt Ethel Mae didn't want to go with us. She said she was all wore out from the trip and needed to rest up. I was right surprised on account of how much she likes shopping. She said she would shop after the trial when she wasn't so worked up. Uncle William gived me some money to buy her a present.

So me and Miss Parker went all by ourselves. I tried on a whole bunch of dresses, and Miss Parker and me chose a navy blue one with a white collar. She said the jury would take me seriously in that dress.

The store also had a whole floor that sold shoes. "Can we just put the shoe beside my foot to see iffen it looks like it will fit?" I asked Miss Parker.

Miss Parker laughed. "I don't think you want to buy shoes that you haven't tried on. You can't tell if they'll be comfortable by looking at them."

"Oh," I said. I took my shoes off. Miss Parker saw the cardboard I had stuffed in them. Then she turned her head away real quick. My face felt hot, and I looked away, too, until the man that tried shoes on my feet asked me how I liked them.

I picked out what the salesman called white patent leather Mary Janes. They was so shiny I could see my face in them. Miss Parker said she thought maybe I should pick out some school shoes, too, just in case my Mary Janes was too tight to wear to the trial.

Then Miss Parker took me to a place in Lazarus that cuts hair. They called it a beauty salon instead of a beauty shop. I got me one of them fancy big-city hairstyles. The woman that cut my hair said she didn't want to take much of it off—that she thought it was real pretty long. She cut bangs in the front and showed me how to use bobby pins to curl them. Then she rolled the ends of my hair in tight little curlers. When my hair dried, I learned how to put it up in a ponytail.

"Lydia, you look like a movie star," Miss Parker said.

When I seen myself in that mirror with all the lights shining down on me, I was real surprised that it was me staring back. I looked real growed up.

Miss Parker bought me three scarves to cover the rubber band when I wore my hair in a ponytail. I picked out a white one that matched the collar of my new dress and a red and a green one to wear to school. I paid for a little bright blue scarf for Aunt Ethel Mae with the money Uncle William gave me. She likes to wear them tied at the side of her neck.

We picked out something nice for Mama to wear, too. Mama's favorite color is green—the color of spring when everthing's fresh and new. So I picked out a light green dress for her. It has skinny brown stripes. We found her a dark brown cardigan sweater the color of hot chocolate, and dark brown shoes to match.

"That's a beautiful dress, Lydia," Miss Parker said. "Your mother will love it. She has such a tiny waist, and the dress will show off her attractive figure." Miss Parker also bought her some makeup, a brown pocketbook that she said Mama would need when she comed home (I liked when she said that), some hankies, and two new pairs of nylon stockings with seams up the back.

I looked through them boxes of stockings, thinking

about what it must be like to be a growed-up lady. I think Miss Parker done read my mind. "Lydia, you're a young lady now," she said. "I think you're too old to wear bobby socks to something as important as a trial—even the pretty ones we bought you to match your dress. Would you like to have your first pair of nylons?"

"Oh, yes!" I said.

She laughed. "It's not as much fun as you think, believe me. You have to be very careful with them so you don't get a run. If we get you a pair of nylons, we have to get you a razor so you can shave your legs. And we can't forget a garter belt."

"I'll be real careful, I promise, but iffen it's too much trouble, I can wear socks." I was sure hoping she didn't think it was too much trouble.

She was already trying to find my size in nylons. "We should get some clear fingernail polish. You can use it to paint your nails, but more importantly, you'll use it to stop a run eventually. All you do is dab a little clear polish around the hole and on the sides of the run."

We stopped by a drugstore, and she bought me a razor, deodorant, clear fingernail polish, and my first tube of light pink lipstick. It's called Blushing Pink, and Miss Parker said it was perfect for someone my age. Miss Parker said I also needed a bag of rubber bands, some bobby pins, and curlers so I could take care of my new hairdo.

I couldn't hardly believe it! My first pair of nylons! And lipstick! When we got back from shopping, Aunt Ethel Mae and Miss Parker and me told Uncle William and

Mr. Hinkle to stay downstairs in the hotel to get something to drink. Then us womenfolk went up to my room so's they could help me with my new things.

Them garter belts sure are weird contraptions! We laughed until our stomachs ached when they tried to teach me how to use that thing. I just about done a dance trying to get them seams in the nylons straight up the backs of my legs.

"Just be thankful you ain't got to wear a girdle, darling," Aunt Ethel Mae told me. "That's something you want to put off as long as possible!"

Miss Parker nodded. "I agree with your aunt on that one, Lydia!"

After I got the hang of using the garter belt, I took them nylons off and put them back in the box. Then they showed me about making up a soap lather to put on my legs and under my arms. They left me alone in the bathroom to give it a try. I took a razor blade out of the little container and placed it inside the razor. Then I screwed the razor up tight. My hands shook just a-thinking about scraping a razor up and down my skin. I let out a few ouches, but it weren't too bad. The more I done it, the easier it got. I wiped off my legs and armpits with a towel and got the bleeding to stop in a few places by pushing on them spots with toilet paper.

Most of the time I just wet a bar of soap and run it up and down my armpits in the mornings to keep them from stinking. This time, I put on the deodorant. "Ouch! It burns!" I said out loud afore I thought.

"What's wrong, Lydia?" Miss Parker asked from outside the door.

"That deodorant hurts!" I told her.

Miss Parker and Aunt Ethel Mae started up laughing. "I'm sorry, Lydia. We should have warned you not to put that on right after you shave your armpits," Miss Parker said.

The burning didn't last too long. I put my clothes back on and looked in the drugstore poke. The lipstick seemed to stare back at me from the bottom of the bag. When I told Aunt Ethel Mae everthing we bought, she said I should only wear the lipstick for special days like Mama's trial. She said she didn't want people thinking I was a hussy, whatever that is. Miss Parker looked at Aunt Ethel Mae kind of strange when she said that, but she didn't say nothing.

I couldn't help myself. I pulled the lipstick out of the poke and held the tube up to my nose to smell it. I thought it would smell like flowers or cherries, but it didn't smell hardly at all. I touched it with my finger. The lipstick felt sticky, sort of like peanut butter. The color was so pretty, like the soft pink roses Gramps had planted for Gran. They blossomed ever year in the spring in back of our house in Paradise. I wished the lipstick smelled like them roses.

I knowed I shouldn't ought to do it, but I stroked the lipstick on my lips and looked at myself in the mirror. My face seemed to be getting a little longer, and my freckles didn't look so dark no more. My hair hung almost to my waist, even after the lady at the beauty salon cut a couple of inches off. I kept thinking about Gran saying I was going to be a looker someday. I wondered iffen a boy might ever say I looked pretty. I thought that might feel right nice iffen he did.

I took one more long look at myself. In six days, I would be twelve years old. All these nice things Miss Parker done for me was like birthday presents—more presents than I ever got in my whole entire life for a birthday or even for Christmas. But I knowed the only thing I really wanted for turning twelve was for Mama to come home. I would give all them presents back for that to happen.

I wiped some soap on the washcloth and scrubbed the lipstick offen my lips. I was real glad the lipstick was a light color, on account of not being able to get it offen the washcloth. I didn't know lipstick stained like that. I folded it up real good so the lipstick didn't show and laid it on the edge of the bathtub. I hoped the hotel didn't make us pay for that washcloth. I felt real bad about that, but I was afeared to let Aunt Ethel Mae and Miss Parker know what I had gone and done.

I walked out of the bathroom, barefoot and with my socks in one hand. "Child, I wondered if you was ever coming out of there," Aunt Ethel Mae said. "Let's see how you did."

I pulled up my skirt a little with my other hand and

turned a circle to show them my hairless legs. They cheered and laughed. "Well done, Lydia," Miss Parker said. "Welcome to womanhood!"

After I put my shoes and socks on, we went downstairs to have supper with Mr. Hinkle and Miss Parker in the hotel cafeteria. I was right surprised to see Jake's mama, Doc Smythson, and Pastor John waiting for us in the lobby. Miss Parker explained that she had invited them to join us. I never expected to see Jake's mama again. Miss Parker introduced everone by their full names—Mrs. Sheila Nowling, Dr. David Smythson, Reverend John Legg, Mr. William Garton, Mrs. Ethel Mae Garton, and Miss Lydia Hawkins.

I wanted to ask Mrs. Nowling about being there, but I didn't think it would be polite. I was just glad to see her again. I sat between her and Miss Parker, but we didn't have a chance to talk afore dinner, 'cause Miss Parker was busy telling people what to expect during the trial.

Miss Parker offered to order for me. I said sure on account of not knowing what a lot of that stuff was on the menu. She ordered me a steak, a baked potato with sour cream, broccoli and cheese, and a salad with Thousand Island dressing. For dessert I had something called Boston cream pie. That Boston cream pie was even better than hot chocolate at Kresge's 5 and 10! At first I thought it was just yellow cake with chocolate icing, but it also had vanilla pudding like Gran used to make in the middle of it. Yum!

I ain't never had steak afore. It was so tender I barely

had to chew— a little salty and real moist. I said a inside thank-you to the cow that gived up its life for my meal. Gran learned me and BJ to do that. Mama said it was on account of Gran's Cherokee blood that she had so much caring for animals and the land. My great-grandmother was a full-blooded Indian. I feel right proud about that.

When we started eating dessert, Jake's mama turned to me. "Lydia, I'm glad you sat beside me," she said. "I have some things I want to tell you. I visited your mother in prison yesterday."

"You got to talk to her?"

"Yes, I visited for as long as they allowed—about twenty minutes."

"What did she say?"

"She wanted me to tell you how much she loves and misses you. Then we talked about what happened to your brother. I told her how sad I was when I read the article about her and BJ. My cousin sent it to me in Alabama. I was so thankful Miss Parker contacted me about coming up here to speak at the new trial. That woman who registered patients at the hospital did the same thing to my husband and me that she did to your family. She told us not to bother reading the contract because we wouldn't be able to understand it."

"What did you do?"

"I skimmed it as quickly as I could, but like your mother, I knew signing that paper, whatever it said, was the only way to get Jake into the hospital. That woman kept sighing, shaking her head, and tapping a pencil while

I tried to read it. When I asked a question, she said, 'Do you want him in the study or not?' I signed. I doubt that she told those rich white folks who came to her office not to read the contract."

"I didn't know that happened to you, too."

"When Jake and BJ were in the hospital together, your mother and I talked about the way that woman treated us. Sarah told Miss Parker about our conversation. I think I'm going to be able to help your mother tomorrow, Lydia."

"Thank you," I said. Afore I thought twice, I scooted my chair back and reached over to hug her.

She hugged me, too. Then she smoothed my hair behind my ear with her hand and smiled at me. I didn't get the ponytail tight enough and some strands of my hair had come out. "You know, Lydia, Jake's sister, Janine, is only a year younger than you. I don't think you ever got to meet her. She always stayed at my cousin's house when we went to the hospital because she was too young to visit Jake. You two have a lot in common."

"We sure do. Just like you and Mama and BJ and Jake."

Mrs. Nowling nodded. "That's true. Your mother and I have so much in common that for a few minutes yesterday we didn't talk at all. She put her hand to the glass that separated us, and I put my hand up to hers, almost touching but not quite. But all that we shared in our hearts connected."

"That sounds real special."

"It was. It meant a lot to both of us, Lydia. We took comfort from each other." She smiled, and then she pulled a piece of paper out of her purse and handed it to me. "I wrote down my daughter's name and address. I thought you might like to write to her. Janine stayed behind with her father so she wouldn't miss school. I'm going to have to leave as soon as the trial is over, so we probably won't have a chance to talk again. I'm a teacher, and I need to get back to my students. I had to stop teaching when we took Jake to Ohio, but the Negro school where I live in Alabama desperately needs qualified teachers. I went back as soon as I could."

"Mr. Hinkle said he read in the newspaper that the Supreme Court is trying to decide whether to make a law that there can't be no more separate Negro schools. He said iffen they pass that law, Negro children and white children will go to school together, the way it always should have been."

"It's going to take schools in the South a long time to abide by that law, Lydia, even if the Supreme Court passes it."

"How come?"

"People are afraid to change ideas and beliefs they grew up with, even when those ideas stem from hate and ignorance."

"I don't see how anybody could hate you, Mrs. Nowling."

"Thank you, Lydia. That's where the ignorance comes in for some people—hating what you don't know or even try to understand."

It was hard for me to figure out what she was saying,

but then I thought about how them doctors and nurses treated BJ and Jake. "It's not just in the South, is it?" I said.

"No, Lydia. Ignorance and hate are diseases that can affect people of all colors and backgrounds. That's why I want to teach—to help children develop skills so that they can overcome whatever obstacles other people try to place in their path. I want them to live happy and fulfilling lives."

"Was it hard to teach kids after losing Jake?" I was thinking about how hard it was for me to see them little tykes at Halloween.

"I think teaching saved me," Mrs. Nowling said, and smiled.

When we finished eating, we walked over to the lobby and sat down in them couches and chairs. No one else was there. Uncle William said, "Excuse me. I need to get something from the car." When he comed back, he had the magic dulcimer wrapped in Gran's sunshine quilt. He laid it on the little table in front of one of the couches. I ain't never been so shocked in all my livelong life!

"Well, come on, Lydia," Uncle William said. "You know I can't play this by myself." He squatted down on the floor on one side of the table. I laughed and sat on the other side. We both said:

> *"Fairies high and fairies low,*
> *Come this day, your powers bestow.*
> *Bring peace and calm and music sure,*
> *Tranquil words and melody pure."*

Then we started up playing and even Aunt Ethel Mae sung along. We told jokes and stories, and sung all evening. People coming in and out of the lobby would stop and listen. Some of them even joined in. The lady at the desk said the hotel should hire us for entertainment. After we went to our rooms, I told Aunt Ethel Mae I was going to use the desk in the lobby to work on some homework. I worked a few math problems so I didn't feel like I lied to her, but then I commenced to write in this here notebook. I want to remember ever single thing that happened today.

I feel all tuckered out but safe and happy—not afeared about tomorrow like I thought I would be. I think I'll get me a good night's sleep, dreaming about seeing my mama again.

28

It's about Mama's new trial.

Today I woke up confident and rested and all ready to speak up for my mama. I sure wish it would have lasted. When I put on my new dress and lipstick and nylons, I felt all growed up and real strong. But later, it was like I had fell deep down into a dark, damp well of them old feelings.

Me and Uncle William and Aunt Ethel Mae ate breakfast at the hotel. Doc Smythson and Pastor John stayed with a friend of Doc's last night. Mrs. Nowling stayed with her cousin. Mr. Hinkle stayed at his parents' house. They live on a farm not too far from here. He planned to drive in early to the city to meet Miss Parker at her parents' house for breakfast. We was all going to meet up at the courthouse at eight. The trial would start up at nine.

I had me some pancakes and orange juice. Aunt Ethel Mae just had toast and hot tea. She kept saying stuff like "I sure do wish we didn't have to go through this today. I feel a headache coming on. I don't know how you're going to deal with all this, Lydia. A young'un shouldn't ought to have to testify. I ain't figured out how I'm going to make myself take that stand without passing out."

Uncle William didn't say nothing. He just kept his eyes on his breakfast of fried eggs, sausage, and biscuits, shoveling the food in his mouth. Sometimes I think Uncle William is deaf, but only when it comes to Aunt Ethel Mae.

The more Aunt Ethel Mae carried on, the more my pancakes started up tasting like rubber. My stomach felt like I was a-swallowing rocks. I finally gived up trying to eat.

Uncle William paid the bill, and then he drove us to the courthouse. We had to drive a piece to get surrounded by all them big buildings. Aunt Ethel Mae was still a-carrying on, but I think I caught Uncle William's deafness to her.

I stared out the window of the car. Ohio is so flat. It's like driving on one of them pancakes I had for breakfast. Gran used to say the sun comed up at your toenails in the morning and set back down on your toenails of an evening when we was in Ohio. It always makes me feel like I don't have no clothes on, driving around up here—like anything bad could come up on me, and I wouldn't have nowhere to hide. Today I wished I was in the mountains again, all safe.

Uncle William let me and Aunt Ethel Mae out in front of the courthouse while he went to park. As we walked inside the door, Aunt Ethel Mae said, "Here we go to face who knows what."

My stomach knotted up tighter inside me.

Miss Parker and everbody else who was here to help my mama was squashed up in a circle at the other end of the big hallway outside the courtroom.

"Over here," Miss Parker called to us, and waved her hand. "Lydia and Ethel Mae, you look beautiful." Miss Parker touched my ponytail and then my shoulder as she smiled at me.

"Do you like my hat?" Aunt Ethel Mae said as she patted it real light. "I added the feathers to make it look like the hats them movie stars wear." I caught myself afore I rolled my eyes like Uncle William always does.

"Uh, it's lovely," Miss Parker said. Then she hurry-up changed the subject. "Reverend Legg has asked if he could lead us in prayer, and I think that's a wonderful idea."

So we all held hands and bowed our heads. Pastor John said his prayer. I didn't hear his words on account of praying my own prayer in my heart. *Please, God. Please let my mama out of that jail. Please, God, please!* I heard Pastor John say amen, and everbody else said amen real long and loud. Me, too.

Then Miss Parker spoke. "We'll be going in soon, and I would like for all of you to sit as close as you can behind Sarah," she said. "We want the jury to see that she has as much support as possible."

"I wish I could sit aside her," I said. I sure did hope she would say I could.

"Lydia, let's sit a minute on this bench," she said. She sent all the other folks on into the courtroom.

We sat down together. "I've thought a lot about this, Lydia," Miss Parker told me. "And I've decided that you will not be in the courtroom until you need to testify."

I felt tears crowding up my eyes. "Please, I want to be close to my mama."

She sighed. "I know you do, Lydia, but the prosecuting attorney is going to do everything he can to make your mother look bad. There's no reason for you to hear it."

"But I done heard it in that other trial. I can handle it this time. I know it."

She sighed again. "It's not a matter of whether you can handle it, Lydia. It's a matter of whether you should hear it. It's going to be worse this time. Your mother's other lawyer was incompetent. The prosecutor knows how skilled I am. He's going to do everything he can to make sure your mother stays in jail."

I looked at the ground. I didn't feel all growed up anymore. I was a little kid again. "I'm the one that be incompetent," I told her. "That's what the judge said. You think so, too."

"Lydia, look at me." I still looked at the ground. "Look at me!" she said louder. She put her finger under my chin and lifted up my face.

I looked at her.

"You know that's not true. You must trust me. It's not just about your having to hear them do that to your mother. You need to think of your mother, too. How do you think she's going to feel, knowing that you're there hearing them say everything they can to make her look bad?"

I looked down at the ground again. "She would feel awful—real sad," I said softly.

"That's right. She doesn't need to be thinking about what's going on with you. She needs to be thinking about her defense."

"I'm sorry. I didn't think about that."

"It's okay, Lydia. I know this is hard. I've arranged a room for you to stay in. It might be several hours before your turn to speak. It might even be tomorrow. I've left a few presents in the room so you'll have something to do while you wait. Come on, I'll show you where you'll be."

We walked down the hallway and she opened the door. I didn't go in. "This is the same room," I told her.

"You mean the same one where they took you during the last trial?"

I nodded.

"It's different this time, Lydia. Last time, this room was filled with fear and despair. This time, let's think of this room being filled with hope. Come see what I have for you."

I followed her. Two packages sat on the table. They was wrapped up with paper covered in flowers and tied up with big pink bows.

"I need to go to the courtroom to be with your mother, Lydia. I know you'll be fine. I'll see you later," Miss Parker said.

"Okay," I told her.

I sat down and unwrapped the first gift. A red diary with a tiny key. The box also had a pencil that doesn't need sharpening. You twist it and the lead comes down the point at the bottom. The package said it's called a mechanical pencil. It also comed with a little box of lead strings to fill it up.

I opened up the diary. In blue ink, Miss Parker had wrote:

To Lydia,
    The strongest young woman I know. May all the dreams you write in this diary come true.

                                    Best wishes,
                                    Julia Parker

I couldn't figure out why she thought I was strong. Maybe she was just trying to be nice. I wrote today's date at the top of the first page. That diary sure was fancier than the spiral notebook I been writing in. I could lock it and not worry about nobody reading it. I'd just have to figure out a safe place to keep the key.

Then I opened up the other package. Two books. *Anne of Green Gables* and *Anne of the Island.* I opened up *Anne of Green Gables.* In blue ink, Mr. Hinkle had wrote:

> *To Lydia,*
>   *I know you have read these books, but I also know Anne is your favorite character. Miss Parker and I thought you would appreciate personal copies. May Anne's courage continue to inspire you.*
>   *Your teacher,*
>   *Mr. Hinkle*

I felt the covers—smooth and velvety. Now I could always have Anne with me. The woody smell of them books remembered me of curling up on my bed in Paradise to read.

I turned to the first page of Anne's first story and read about the most important day in her life. The day when she left all the bad behind, all the TRAGICAL, she called it, and started up all the good things with Matthew and Marilla.

I was thankful I had Anne to keep me company on my most important day. I sure hoped I could leave all the TRAGICAL behind. I joined Anne in her life so's I could forget about what was going on in mine.

When I first sat down at the table, the clock in the room seemed loud, clicking by the minutes. But I was surprised when Miss Parker walked in to get me. I looked up at the clock and it was already eleven-thirty. I had read almost half of my book.

"Lydia," she said, "you're next to testify. I asked the judge if we could take a recess for lunch before you're called to the stand. We need to be back at one. I thought you and I would go to lunch together. There's a sandwich shop down the street."

We walked to the shop and ordered hamburgers and French fries. Miss Parker asked for a cup of coffee, and I asked for a root beer. When the waitress handed us our drinks, I told Miss Parker about BJ putting raisins in the root beer back in Paradise. The two of us had a good laugh over that one. She told me about how when she was little, her brother asked her iffen she wanted half of his peanut butter sandwich. She said yes. When she took a bite, she bit off the head of a water bug he had stuffed inside. Us women decided that boys sure do weird things sometimes.

After we finished eating, we talked about what was going to happen next. She asked me iffen I recollected all the things she had taught me about trials afore Christmas. I told her yes.

Miss Parker already learned me all them big words that lawyers and judges use. She said that Mama is the defendant because she needs defending. BJ's hospital is the plaintiff on account of them doctors complaining about Mama taking BJ out of the hospital.

Attorney is just a fancy word for lawyer. Miss Parker is the defense attorney because she defends Mama. The

233

lawyer who tries to make Mama look guilty of doing something wrong is the prosecuting attorney. I told Miss Parker I thought he should be called the persecuting attorney. She said in Mama's case, she agreed with me.

The jury is a group of people that listen real close to everthing that everybody says. When the lawyers finish up saying everthing they want to say, they go out to another room to decide iffen the defendant is guilty or not guilty of doing a bad thing. Iffen they say *guilty*, the judge decides what the punishment should be. Iffen they say *not guilty*, everybody gets to go home, including the defendant. I hope that's what happens to my mama, that the jury figures out she's not guilty, and we all get to go home to West Virginia.

When Miss Parker got done learning me all that lawyering stuff, she said I was just about ready to pass the bar—that's a big test people take after they get all their book learning to prove they's ready to be lawyers.

I also learned that swearing on the Bible in court means saying that you promise to God and everbody else that you ain't going to lie. And as long as you don't tell a lie, God will be right proud of you.

After I finished up reminding her of what she learned me, Miss Parker nodded. "Good. I'm glad you remember," she said. "I've helped you understand the basics, but I want to tell you what the prosecuting attorney might ask you. He'll want to know what your mother had you do to help get your brother out of the hospital. He'll want to make the jury think that your mother forced you to do something that you shouldn't have done. I can't help you practice what to say. That should come straight from your heart. Keep your answers honest, short, and to the point. When he finishes, I'll ask you some questions to give you a chance to explain more. Do you understand?"

I nodded.

"When I ask you questions, the prosecuting attorney might try to interrupt you and say that he objects to what you are saying or the questions I ask. Don't worry about him. I'll take care of any interruptions he tries to make. We'll find a way for you to say everything you want to say about your mother and your brother. And if he starts asking you questions that I don't think are appropriate, I will interrupt him with an objection. He's tough, Lydia. But all you need to be concerned about is telling the truth."

When we walked back to the courthouse, I thought about what I would say. I would tell what I done to help Mama get BJ out of the hospital. I would tell about how BJ cried when Gran died on account of her not having any kin with her. And I would say that I remembered Mama of that and begged her to bring BJ home. Then I would ask all them people how Mama and I could *not* bring him home to die with us iffen we loved him.

So I thought I was ready. But when I walked in that big room again with all them important people, it was like I was having a nightmare and was back in Mama's first trial. I looked at the twelve empty seats at the side of the courtroom, waiting for the judge to call in twelve strangers that would look at me like I might be a criminal. I knowed from what Miss Parker told me that they was the jury. Them people was going to decide what happened to my mama. And by deciding what happened to my mama, they was going to decide what happened to me. All at once I felt dizzy and as jumpy as a grasshopper in a henhouse.

Then I saw them people in uniforms bring in my mama—in handcuffs. Her long hair had been cut short. Her beautiful hair was gone. The dress Miss Parker and me picked out for her was too big. She looked like a little girl playing dress-up in it. Mama walked to her seat without looking up from the floor. Didn't she know I was in the room? Why didn't she look for me? Did she know that Uncle William told me the truth about him and Helen? Was she too ashamed? Did she still love me?

The room started spinning and Uncle William had to catch me. He sat me down on a bench. Miss Parker runned over.

"Is Lydia all right?" Miss Parker asked my uncle. "Maybe we're expecting too much of her." She looked at me, her eyebrows arched up high, all worried-like. "Dr. Smythson is still outside with the pastor. I'll go get him."

"She'll be fine," Uncle William said. "You just go on and do the lawyering you need to do with Sarah. I'll tend to Lydia."

Miss Parker looked at Uncle William like she weren't too sure whether to leave me, but then she went to Mama's side.

Uncle William sat down beside me. I smelled bacca on

him and knowed he had hisself a smoke after lunch. He didn't look at me when he talked. "Lydia, this sure has been a hard road for you to travel, but you got good blood running through your veins. Never forget who you be."

Then he went to talk to Doc Smythson and Pastor John and left me alone.

I recollected Mama saying them very same words to me. "Never forget who you be." Them was the last words she said to me afore Doc Smythson took me away from Paradise.

Uncle William and Mama knowed that I ain't who I thought I was. It didn't make no sense that they said that to me. What did Uncle William mean about good blood? But then I got to thinking that maybe they was saying I be more than who my mama and daddy be. That my blood runs deeper than that.

I recollected about how I felt when we drove to the courthouse—wishing I was back in the mountains. I figured something out. Them mountains is always and forever inside of me, making me who I be. My blood is like a river running through them mountains. As sure as I feel this here chair I'm sitting in right now, at the trial I felt them mountains filling up all the empty spaces inside me. Gran, Gramps, Mama, Daddy, BJ, Uncle William, Helen, and even Aunt Ethel Mae. The blood of them mountains flowed deep in all of us.

Gran always said our West Virginia mountains is like the bosom of the Almighty, keeping us protected and still in Him. That brought to mind one of them Bible verses Gran made me learn by heart. *I will lift up mine eyes unto the hills, from whence cometh my help. My help cometh from the Lord, the maker of Heaven and Earth.*

And when I looked to them hills I always carry deep inside, I felt their strength. And I felt God, who made them hills, inside of me, too. Maybe the truth of who I really be had set me free after all.

I didn't even notice Doc Smythson standing beside me. He knelt down and looked in my eyes. "How are you doing, Lydia?" he asked, all worried. "Let me feel your pulse."

I held my arm out to him. "I feel better," I told him.

He looked at his watch and counted the beats. "Nice and strong," he said, and winked at me.

"All rise!" a man shouted. We all stood up while the judge walked in and sat down. The judge remembered me of a bulldog that belonged to our neighbor in Paradise. He had saggy jowls and his face was shaped like a rectangle. He looked like he might growl. I was mighty afeared of that bulldog at first, but after we got to know each other, he turned out to be a pretty good dog. I hoped this judge would turn out to be nicer than he looked, too.

The judge called in the jury. Then we all sat down after the judge took his seat.

"The prosecution calls Lydia Hawkins, Your Honor," the hospital's lawyer boomed out. As I walked to the front of the courtroom, I looked over and saw my mama smile at me. She was skinny and had lost her beautiful long hair, but her eyes was just the same—blue and clear and strong.

The man that had us stand up when the judge walked in told me to place my left hand on the Bible and raise my right hand. Then he said, "Do you solemnly swear before almighty God, the seeker of all hearts, to tell the truth, the whole truth, and nothing but the truth, as you will so answer on that last great day?"

I looked him in the eye and smiled. "I swear," I said.

29

It's about being in Paradise.

SATURDAY, APRIL 3, 1954

Me and Mama sat in the rocking chairs out on the porch today. Ears sat beside me with his big old head in my lap. I rested my elbows on the arms of the rocking chair so's I could sew over the top of his head. The sun cozied up to us and spring finally started to peek out of the ground and the trees. The sweet smell of honeysuckle blowed a kiss to us from the side of the house.

We sewed memory quilts for BJ and Gran. Mama tore up strips out of my old coat to use for the border of Gran's quilt. I sewed a train on BJ's quilt that looked like the magic train. I cut me up some root beer jars out of BJ's old brown britches. Then I sewed together two of his black socks to make a long black snake. It had a red forked tongue from one of his baby bibs. I cut the letters *G, E, R, M, Y* out of his black-and-red plaid shirt to sew under the snake. I figured BJ was laughing up there in Heaven about having root beer jars and a black snake on his quilt. It made me smile just to think about it.

I stopped for a minute to scratch behind Ears' ears. He looked up at me real grateful-like.

"Mama, it sure was nice of Aunt Ethel Mae to talk her neighbor into letting me have Ears. I still ain't figured out why she done that. She was always a-telling me what a awful, smelly old dog he was."

Mama laughed. It sounded like little bells ringing. I felt all warm and peaceful, hearing her laugh again. "Well, Lydia, look at it this way," she said. "She managed to get the dog out of her neighborhood."

I laughed, too. "Aunt Ethel Mae could talk anybody into anything," I said.

"That's for sure and certain," Mama agreed. "That poor neighbor didn't have no chance against your aunt." Mama patted Ears on the head. He looked at her and wagged his tail. Then Mama patted my hand. "You know, Lydia, your aunt and uncle love you very much. I'm sure they miss having you with them."

I stopped sewing and looked down at the ground. "Mama, why can't I tell nobody that Uncle William is my birth father?"

Mama sighed—not a I-can't-believe-you-said-that sigh, but like she let go of a real heavy burden.

She lifted the quilt offen her lap and laid it in the

basket next to her. "Lydia, I been waiting for you to bring it up. William said he told you. I wanted our talk about this to be when you was ready."

Mama looked at my face. I finally turned to look at her. She had tears in her eyes. "I be so sorry we kept the truth from you, Lydia. Your gran and William and me—we never wanted you to find out the way you did."

"Why didn't you tell me, Mama?"

"It was such a hard thing to explain, Lydia. You seemed too young to be able to grasp things about war and death when you first asked about being borned. Your gran said she told you about coming out of me real easy. I was upset with her, Lydia. I figured it would make the truth harder for you to accept later on. I told her so, but she said, 'Land sakes, Sarah, what on earth did you expect me to say when that little thing asked such a question?'"

I grinned a little. I could hear Gran saying that. The me-missing-her part sure was a whole lot bigger than the me-being-mad-at-her part. "Why didn't you tell me when I got older?" I asked.

"I don't know, Lydia. The timing never seemed right, and it was important that you not tell. Then BJ got so sick. I kept thinking in that prison cell that I wished I would have told you afore I got tooken away."

I looked down at the ground again. "Mama, did you love BJ more than me? You birthed him." Tears pushed out of my eyes, and I wiped them away with my hand.

Mama stood up. "Come here to me," she said. I laid my quilting down. She real gentle pulled me up by the arm and sat down again, tugging me toward her. "Sit on my lap, Lydia."

"No, Mama. I'm too big for that. I might hurt you."

"Just this once, Lydia. Sit on my lap. I'm a lot stronger than I look." She winked at me and patted her lap.

I sat down as soft as I could. She wrapped her arms around me, and I wrapped my arms around her. She held me like I weren't much more than a baby.

"I dreamed of this day, Lydia, the whole time I was in that there prison—the day I could hold you in my arms again, my daughter," Mama whispered to me.

Ears laid his head on my lap and pushed Mama's hand with his nose to get some loving, too. We couldn't help but laugh at him.

We sat that way for a time, the three of us, and then Mama said, "Your daddy wasn't drinking back when William asked us to take you. We didn't just take you to help William out. We was thrilled to have us a baby girl in our home. You don't know how often I watched you sleep at night and thanked God for giving me such a precious gift. I couldn't love you or BJ one more than the other. I always loved both of you as much as my heart can love."

And I believed her on account of feeling how powerful her love for me was in the way she held me. She kissed me on the forehead.

I could have stayed on her lap forever, but I figured I must be getting heavy. I got up and sat back down in my rocking chair. Ears plopped down beside me to take a nap. Mama and me both picked up our quilting again and commenced to sew. "Why can't I tell no one, Mama?" I asked.

"There's something I never told you about your aunt Ethel Mae," Mama said. "You're getting on to be a woman, now. I think you deserve to know the truth about everthing."

I couldn't imagine what I didn't know about Aunt Ethel Mae. I had me about all the truth I thought I could handle. But I asked anyways. "What's that, Mama?"

"Your aunt wanted real bad to have young'uns of her own. William thought he was ready to start his own family, too. Your aunt was with child twice, but she couldn't carry the baby either time. After she lost the second baby, the doctor said he didn't have no choice but to take out her woman's parts."

"Oh, Mama, that's terrible!"

"Yes, it's right sad. Your aunt said she felt all dried up and useless after that. I think that might be why she's so sickly all the time with them bad headaches and all. She turned that sad inside on herself. Them women parts is real important to how you feel about yourself and the world, Lydia."

"Will her sad ever go away, Mama?"

"No more than our sad about Gran and BJ. But I been noticing that she ain't complaining as much about headaches lately."

"I have, too, Mama."

"I think you might have helped her find out that she still has room for joy, even with the sad."

"Like Gran used to tell us?"

"Just exactly like Gran used to tell us. 'We can't let our sad rob us of our joy.'"

"Iffen she's doing better, why can't we tell her?"

"William and me was afeared that she might want to try to take you as her daughter, Lydia," Mama said. "She wanted kids real bad, and she's so fond of you. And you know how she is when she wants something."

My chest got tight. "No, Mama. I want to stay with you."

"William and me think that's best, too, Lydia. Him and me talked about this a lot since I got home. We wanted you to talk to me and ask your questions first, and we knowed that you would ask when you was ready to hear. Now that you and me talked, William and me will tell Ethel Mae the truth. No more family secrets. It ain't fair for you to have to hide, Lydia. Secrets cause shame, and I never ever want you to feel shame."

I know my eyes was real wide. "But, Mama," I said. "I don't want to have to live with Uncle William and Aunt Ethel Mae. I love them for what they done for me when you was gone. They's always going to be special to me. But I want to live with you."

"William and me will work it out, Lydia. We are all family, and we'll find a way. I have your adoption papers. We know it's best for you to stay with me, and I think your aunt will come to understand that, too."

I sure hoped she was right. Iffen we wasn't going to have no more family secrets, I figured I best tell her my secret. "Mama," I said without looking up from my sewing, "I went to the cemetery to see where Helen was buried."

She didn't say nothing for a minute. "Good, Lydia," she finally said. "I'm glad you done that. You two are joined by birth. How was it for you?"

"I skipped school to go. I told Mr. Hinkle I was sick. I lied, Mama."

Mama nodded. She didn't look mad at all. "After we tell Ethel Mae, you can explain to Mr. Hinkle. I'm sure he'll understand."

Then I nodded. After all me and Mr. Hinkle been through together, I figured he understood me as good as most anybody. "I took Ears with me," I told Mama. "It was pretty there. And peaceful. I talked to Helen the best I could. But I called her Helen. You're my mama." Mama smiled at me and patted my hand. I wanted to tell her something else. "On her headstone, there was a verse. *My spirit frees, and I am one with God.* I don't recollect that from the Bible."

"It's from one of her poems. Helen was a wonderful woman, Lydia. You could feel how much she loved people and life in what she wrote. And she had this great laugh— real hearty. Not something you would expect to come out of such a tiny woman. We didn't get together with William and Helen too much, but her and me was becoming good friends. I miss her."

"Does Uncle William still have her poems and stories?"

"You'll have to ask him, Lydia. I don't know."

"Do you think she can see me from Heaven, Mama?"

"I think her and BJ and Gran probably talk about how proud they be of you all the time, Lydia. And I'm sure Helen tells them that she believes you was the best thing she ever done with her life."

We sat quiet for a spell as we rocked and sewed, rocked and sewed. Then I thought of something else I wanted to talk to her about.

"Mama," I said, "I been thinking some about what Mr. Hinkle told me one time about having a dream for my future. I think me and Anne of Green Gables sure do have us a lot in common."

"Why is that, Lydia?" Mama asked.

"I want to be a teacher someday, too—a real good one like Anne and Mr. Hinkle and Mrs. Nowling."

"That sounds like a mighty fine dream, Lydia. Sheila told me her family didn't have no money to help her, but she worked hard to put herself through college. Iffen she done it, I believe you can, too."

"I will, Mama. I just know it. You know that letter I got from Janine the other day? She said she wants to be a teacher, too. I finally found me a person friend who's a kindred spirit like Anne Shirley had. Maybe me and Janine can go to college together. It sure would be fun iffen we could be roommates."

"Maybe by the time you both are old enough, it will be possible to go to college together. I think things be changing in this country. And some of them changes be real good."

I thought on that for a while. "Miss Parker said when

you win your civil trial that you'll have more money than you ever had," I said. "Are we going to be rich?"

Mama winked at me. "We always been rich, Lydia. We just ain't had much money. I don't know what to do about that yet. It don't seem right to sue a children's hospital. Miss Parker says we need to make sure they stop treating people like they treated us, and sometimes the only way to do that is by a lawsuit. She said maybe we could get a settlement. I don't know, Lydia. I'll have to keep studying on it."

We rocked and sewed, rocked and sewed some more. Then I said, "Mama, there's something I been pondering about for a long time."

Mama threaded herself up a needle. "What's that, Lydia?"

"How come you and Gran and BJ was always so strong going through all that bad stuff, and I was so weak?"

Mama looked up at me, her eyes all wide. She stopped rocking and put her hand on my arm. "Oh, Lydia," she said. "Do you really believe that?"

"Yes, Mama. I was always a-crying and a-feeling like I was going to fall to pieces."

Mama smiled and patted my arm. "Here is a Gran test for you, Lydia. What's the shortest verse in the Bible?"

"'*Jesus wept*,'" I said without even thinking. Then I smiled.

"I done my share of crying and falling to pieces, too, Lydia, especially in that jail, thinking about what you must be going through without me."

"You did, Mama?"

"Um-hum." She went back to rocking and sewing. "But I come to think that being strong ain't about being tough or holding things all bottled up inside when you have real bad times. It's just about leaning on Jesus and the folks He puts around you and putting one foot in front of the other until you cross over into some better days. You done that just fine, Lydia."

I studied on them words for a spell. "But, Mama, what about when I was so weak and afeared that I couldn't speak up for you at that first trial?" Some tears flooded up my eyes.

Mama tied a knot in her row and bit off the thread. "Lydia, I was never so proud of you as I was at that moment."

"But why, Mama?"

"I figured out you thought it was wrong to swear on the Bible. And I said to myself, Lydia is always going to do what she believes is right, no matter what. And then I didn't feel so afeared for you anymore. I knowed you would always be a strong voice in this world."

We listened to the thoughts inside us for a while. Then Mama broke the silence. "It's a little chilly out here, don't you think?" she said. She put her needle down and pulled her sweater around her. Then she balled up her right hand in a fist and rested it on the arm of the rocking chair. She rubbed her thumb over her fingers to get them warm.

I laid my hand over hers. "Paper covers rock," I said.

Mama grinned at me and I grinned back.

AUTHOR'S NOTE

I am a child of the mountains. West Virginia has been home to ancestors on both sides of my family since the late seventeen hundreds. My father's family, originally named Schenck, emigrated to the United States from Switzerland, Germany, and England. Some of my mother's family also came from England, but others came from France and Italy. My great-great-grandmother on my mother's side was Cherokee, and like Lydia, "I'm right proud of that."

Ancestors from both families eventually settled in the section of Virginia that became West Virginia during the Civil War. I have distant relatives who fought on both sides of the war that pitted brother against brother. Most Virginians who lived west of the Appalachian Mountains aligned with the Union, and delegates to the Wheeling Convention in what became known as West Virginia Independence Hall voted to secede from Virginia. President Abraham Lincoln signed a proclamation that granted West Virginia statehood on June 20, 1863.

Some of the Schencks were Mennonites fleeing religious persecution in Europe. After one of my father's ancestors was excommunicated in the United States for marrying outside the Mennonite community, he became Baptist, a faith he passed to many of his descendants. The deep faith treasured by many Appalachians, myself included, probably stems from ancestors who were willing to sacrifice everything for their beliefs.

My father's family lived on Paradise Hill in Putnam County and later moved to Kanawha County. Many of my mother's ancestors settled in Jackson and Mason counties, and some eventually took flatboats to Kanawha County, where my parents met and I was born. I grew up in Charleston, the urban capital of West Virginia, but I loved to visit relatives in the country.

People in Putnam County like to say, "You have to go through Confidence and Liberty before you get to Paradise," using those three towns as a metaphor for life. Although Confidence was never a coal camp, I chose it to symbolize Lydia's need to find confidence in her faith and her sense of self before she could return to Paradise.

Some of the scenes in *Child of the Mountains* reflect real-life events. My father, his four brothers, and their sons turned intellectual curiosity into mischief when they were kids, much as BJ did. For example, my uncle Lowell slipped raisins into jars of his mother's homemade root beer to see if they would ferment. And yes, the jars exploded.

The voices of Lydia and her family mirror those of my childhood. Friends and relatives I loved and respected spoke the lyrical language of the hills. Many of Gran's sayings come from my father, a scientist, who loved Appalachian metaphor and wit. My mother switched easily from Appalachian dialect to standard English, depending on the people around her. And to this day, if you get me riled up, you just might hear me say something like "I ain't never going to do that, no way, nohow!"

I haven't always felt comfortable with the dialect of my heritage. I stopped saying "boosh" and "poosh" for *bush* and *push* and "feeshin'" for *fishing* when I tired of the teasing in college. No doubt I lost something important when I changed who I was for other people. So when I think of the young woman Lydia will become, I believe she too will struggle with her identity as her circumstances change.

Historically, West Virginians were an open, trusting people. However, when coal companies hired outlanders to rob West Virginians of their land and exploit the state's resources for personal gain, mistrust of those outside the region grew. Not only West Virginians but Appalachians in general tend to value close bonds with family, friends, and neighbors. They will lend a helping hand when someone is in need, just as Lydia's family reached out to others.

I chose to set *Child of the Mountains* during the year I was born. As I began researching the year 1953, I discovered that my decision was appropriate for the story. West Virginia experienced a severe drought that year, which seemed to reflect the drought Lydia experienced in her life. The polio epidemic also reached its peak then, with so many children hospitalized that beds had to be placed in hallways, as in an important scene in the novel.

I was hospitalized twice as a child during the 1950s and remember only one compassionate nurse. Doctors and nurses seemed to be concerned only about disease and running an orderly hospital, not about the emotional needs of a frightened child. Doctors stood around my bed daily and talked about me but not to me. BJ has the same experience during his stays in the hospital. I'm thankful that today, children's research hospitals, unlike the fictional hospital in the story, are more sensitive to patients' and families' need for support.

William Casey Marland was governor of West Virginia from 1952 to 1956. He tried to establish a severance tax on natural resources, including coal, of ten cents per ton, which would have greatly enhanced the state's economy and helped improve highways and schools. The legislature was heavily influenced by the coal industry, however, so the tax didn't pass. Marland also worked hard to implement desegregation in West Virginia after the 1954 Supreme Court decision *Brown v. Board of Education,* which Lydia's teacher discusses in class.

I benefitted from that governor's efforts. An early attempt at desegregation involved placing African American teachers in schools with mostly European American students. My fourth-grade teacher, Mrs. Bette Nowling, was one of those teachers. You will find her mentioned in the acknowledgments, and I chose her last name for Jake's family.

Given the deep ties I have to West Virginia, I'm not surprised that one day, while I was home in Alabama, sitting at my computer preparing lessons for my college students, I heard a girl's West Virginia voice in my head say, "My mama's in jail. It ain't right." I tried to return to my work, but the voice persisted. I finally opened a new file and wrote the first page of what I originally titled *Paper Covers Rock*. At the time, I had no idea that the small voice I heard would become *Child of the Mountains*.

The poverty Lydia's family experiences is still rampant in many parts of West Virginia and throughout Appalachia. Tragically, some young people are turning to drugs, alcohol, and even suicide to escape extraordinarily challenging circumstances. It's my hope that, like Lydia, children of the mountains will find the faith and courage they need to sustain them through difficult times, remembering that better days will come. And if they require help, people will be there for them. They only need to ask.

Montani semper liberi.

ACKNOWLEDGMENTS

Thank you to:

My agent, Christine Witthohn of Book Cents Literary Agency, for guiding me through the editing and publishing process with unwavering support and belief in this manuscript.

My editor, Françoise Bui, for embracing Appalachia and helping this manuscript achieve its potential.

Copy editor Joy Simpkins, a fellow West Virginian, for maintaining the integrity of the characters' dialect and voices.

My niece Jennifer Wilkes and nephew Matthew Shank for sharing their West Virginia childhoods with me.

My cousin Gary Shank, whose timely phone calls reminded

me of this novel's purpose and motivated me to stay focused to complete it.

The BC Babes and Guys, writers extraordinaire, for encouragement, helpful suggestions, and a few laughs.

Extended family, especially Elsie Borsch, Betty Slater, Sarah Roberts, Lucian and Betty Shank, Lorene Shank, and Louise Steele, for sharing their West Virginia recollections. Other family and friends, especially Kathy Shank, Charles Borsch, Sarah Kroemer, Debbie Petry, Cindy Rango, Jim and Terry Sue Shank, Roberta Shank, Terry Shank, William and Wanda Shank, Dot Sheely, Pat and Kay Seaton, Mike Slater, Joe and Kim Trotta, Martha Adams, Ralph and Mary Allison, Mehrzad Araghi, Sandy Barker, Linda Bishop, Jo Blackwood, Bettie Bullard, Müzeyyen Çiyiltepe, Jim and Suzy Efaw, Sue Forsbrey, Ross Harrison, Diann Hindman, Barbara Holmes, Jimmy Jones, Bill and Dorothy Leal, John MacCallum, Catherine Moore, Joyce McNeill, Gilbert and Sandra McClanahan, Donna Rogers, Sandy Tritt, Debbie Troxclair, Rud and Ann Turnbull, and Carolyn Whitlock, for their encouragement and support of my writing and during challenging times.

The McClarahans and the Shamblins, for exemplifying what it means to be good neighbors.

Members and conference faculty of the Society of Children's Book Writers and Illustrators, especially Joan Broerman, Anne Dalton, Jo Kittinger, and Han Nolan for teaching, inspiring, and sometimes cajoling me.

258

Barbara Kouts for her support during a crucial phase in the manuscript.

The Highlights Foundation for the scholarship to Chautauqua, an experience that helped me believe in myself as a writer.

Faculty and participants of the 2003 Highlights Chautauqua Conference, especially faculty member Patricia Gauch; my mentor, Dayton Hyde; and my roommate, Linda Lyman, who were in the right place at the right time to touch my life and enrich my writing.

District Magistrate Charles Conway for use of his swearing-in statement and for providing helpful recommendations.

Kyle Edwards, for telling me what it feels like to have sickle-cell disease.

Librarians at the West Virginia Cultural Center, Columbus Metropolitan Library, Kanawha County Public Library, Cross Lanes Public Library, South Charleston Public Library, and Putnam County Public Library for answering numerous questions and guiding me toward important research.

My fourth-grade teacher, Bette Nowling, for telling me she loved to read my stories.

ABOUT THE AUTHOR

Marilyn Sue Shank, a proud West Virginian, earned her PhD in special education from the University of Kansas, where she majored in learning disabilities and behavior disorders and minored in counseling psychology and families with disabilities. She has taught general and special education at the elementary, secondary, and college levels.

Marilyn's work has been published in professional journals, and she coauthored the first four editions of *Exceptional Lives: Special Education in Today's Schools*. *Child of the Mountains* is her first work of fiction. She lives in West Virginia with her three rescued dogs, including one named Ears.